TOME TO TOMB

ST. MARIN'S COZY MYSTERY 5

ACF BOOKENS

1

My memories of Santa Claus are scant. For a few years when I was little, extra toys appeared on Christmas morning, and a couple of times, the cookies got eaten, too. I expect Mom and Dad took me to the mall or some such place to sit on the lap of the guy in the red suit, too. But my most vivid memory associated with Santa was finding my presents from Santa in my grandfather's car one December. The magic ended there . . . at least as far as Santa was concerned.

But I've always loved Christmas. As a kid, I loved the church Christmas pageants and the Midnight Candlelight Service on Christmas Eve. I adored driving around and looking at the lights on all the houses, and the Grinch always made an appearance on an evening when I got to stay up late with a big, marshmallow-laden cup of hot cocoa and watch TV in my pajamas. But by far, my favorite part of Christmas was the people. Mom always had charity parties at our house, and Dad made sure his firm had a kid-friendly holiday gathering. I loved them all, even though I often sat in the corner and dipped in and out of my current book while people swirled around me. I was introverted as a kid, but I was also a lover of people, at least people watching.

Which is why when I learned that St. Marin's had been without its decades-long tradition of having Santa greet children on Main Street, I agreed to host. Santa had been absent last year, and while I hadn't known why our little business district had felt a bit wan, it now was clear that Santa's absence was the cause. Apparently, the Chamber of Commerce had always set up Santa's cottage in the old gas station that was now my bookstore, but they'd felt awkward about asking me if they could use the space when I'd taken it over a little over a year back. And apparently, the town couldn't quite figure out what to do instead, so no Santa.

This year, though, an entire front corner of the bookstore was going to be Santa's workshop, and he would be on hand every weekend in December to greet our youngest (and our most fun-loving older) guests and hear their Christmas wishes.

The trouble was that my staff and I were in a stalemate over what we should call the space where Santa would be. My assistant manager, Marcus, wanted to call it the Santa Zone because, as he said, it would be a tip of the hat to Frozone, his favorite character from *The Incredibles* movies. I liked that idea, especially because our Santa was going to be black, like the character voiced by Samuel L. Jackson in the movies, but it also reminded me of some sort of sports/arcade/game complex, and I really didn't want to send the wrong signal about the kind of experience people were going to have.

Rocky, Marcus' girlfriend and the café manager, had suggested Santa's Village, but Marcus had quashed that idea because it felt confusing to him to have a village within a village, which is basically what our town is. I wouldn't have thought of that dilemma myself, but once he said it, I couldn't help going all meta and imagining Santa in some sort of

Escher-like reality where a series of ever-smaller villages sat inside of each other infinitely.

My idea was to go with the classic cottage motif the town had always used, but Rocky and Marcus both said that didn't work because he wasn't really going to have a cottage per se. I briefly wondered about having our friend Woody, the woodsmith, make us a cottage to put in the front of the store, but the logistics of moving around something that big in our small shop made that a no-go. So we were stuck.

And on the Monday before Thanksgiving, we had just five days to decide on a name, make the signs, advertise, and decorate before Santa came for his first evening in the shop on Friday. The three of us were staring into space at one of the café tables, trying to come up with a solution, and it was looking more and more futile. The shop was opening in fifteen minutes, and I felt like we had to decide something this morning. We had to pick something, and we'd put it off for as long as we could.

"What if the sign just said, 'Come see Santa?'" Marcus suggested. "Utilitarian but clear."

Rocky sighed. "I guess that would work." She looked at me forlornly.

I echoed her sigh and glanced out the window just in time to see our friend Elle Heron drive by with a child's sled strapped to the top of her minivan. That's when it hit me.

"Santa's Sleigh." I almost whispered.

"What?" Rocky said as she placed her light brown hand over mine. "What did you say?"

I looked from her to Marcus and back. "Santa's Sleigh. What if we set Santa up in a sleigh instead of a chair? That way children could sit next to him if they didn't want to sit on his lap."

Rocky nodded. "Oh, I like that. We want to be sure to keep kids comfortable, and I've always wondered what telling chil-

dren to sit on a strange man's lap teaches them about their right
to say no when it comes to their bodies."

"I agree," and felt my enthusiasm rising as I imagined a
bright red sleigh and some Christmas trees around it with that
fake snow that had glitter in it. I was just to the point of
thinking about how we could string simple white lights around
the sleigh to make it light up the store window at night when I
caught the expression on Marcus's face. "Oh no. You don't
like it?"

He met my gaze. "No, I love it, but I'm remembering this
Hallmark movie where—"

"Did you say Hallmark Movie?" I smirked.

"Seriously, there's nothing better to put you in the holiday
spirit," he said without a hint of irony. "Great décor, a guaran-
teed happy ending, and just enough drama to keep you
interested."

Rocky winked at me. "He's the only black man I know who
watches more of them than I do."

"Forget the fact that he's black. He's the only man I know
who watches them at all," I laughed as Marcus rolled his eyes.
"But you were saying something about a Hallmark movie?" I
stuck my tongue out at him.

"I was saying that there's this one movie where they have to
find a sleigh for some event at an inn, I think, and they can't
find one. Those movies aren't very realistic, but well, that part
seems to me as true to life. Where are we going to get a sleigh?"

I felt my excitement deflate. "Good question." I stood up.
"Visit Santa it is," I said as I headed toward the front of the
store, flicked on the open sign, and turned the lock on the door.
I tried to counter my disappointment with the excitement I felt
about hosting Santa, period. But I was still thinking about the
sleigh.

Just then, the bell over the front door rang, and Galen – my
favorite customer – came in with his English bulldog, Mack.

My hound, Mayhem, quickly jogged over, gave Mack the sniff of greeting, and promptly led him to the new couch-shaped dog bed in the fiction section. Galen was always getting doggy goodies because of his Instagram account that featured books and dogs. Apparently, he got so much that he couldn't fit everything in his house, so he gave a lot of it away. For a while, I'd been a grateful beneficiary, but a couple of weeks ago, I'd had to tell him that we now had enough luxury dog beds to sleep a hundred dogs and that we had to keep some room for books.

"I was wondering when you'd hit saturation," Galen said with a smile. "Good thing I already lined up my next recipients. Did you know that Cate is now allowing dogs at the co-op?"

My good friend Cate was a photographer and the owner of the amazing art co-op at the other end of Main Street. Her dog, Sasquatch, was another of Mayhem's buds. "I didn't know that. I thought she was worried about fur in the clay and the paint and such."

"She was, but then Sasquatch was feeling sick one day and had to come to work with her. She put his doggy bed in the window, and their traffic doubled. So she polled the artists. Turns out, everyone was in favor." Galen grinned as he looked over at Mayhem and Mack, who were butt to butt on their couch.

"I told her, but I guess she had to see for herself." A good portion of our foot traffic came in because the dogs especially loved the sunshine in the front windows in the afternoon. "I'm glad you can pass along your goodies to someone else. You have a lot of space there, too."

"Yep, one bed per artist and a few for the lobby, I figure." Galen was staring over at Mack with such gentle adoration. Dog people were special, and not all of us carried our dogs in purses . . . although I couldn't really resist those teacup chihuahuas that customers brought in from time to time.

"So what's new around here? Anything you want me to Insta for the holidays?"

I groaned audibly and Galen raised his eyebrows. "We were just talking about that. Santa is going to be here for the weekends starting this Friday, but we haven't figured out what to call his, well, place." I sighed. "Cottage doesn't work, and village feels weird. We talked about a sleigh, but then we couldn't figure out how to get a sleigh—"

"I have a sleigh you can use."

"So we're going with a sign that says – wait, what?!" It took my brain a few seconds to stop my mouth. "Did you say you have a sleigh?"

"Yep. I put it in the front yard with a bunch of life-sized stuffed dogs to pull it, but I'm kind of tired of hauling the thing out, and last year, a squirrel made a nest in the Great Pyrenees belly. So I wasn't planning on using it this year. It's yours if you want it."

I stared at Galen for a long moment, picturing the sleigh with a dog team pulling it and then the squirrel climbing out of a fake Great Pyr belly before I finally registered that he had just solved our problem. "Really?! That would be amazing. Are you sure?"

"Absolutely. Maybe Daniel can come by and get it?" Galen said.

"Sure. I mean I'll ask, but I expect he'd be happy to. Will it fit in my truck?" I drove an old model Chevy, and I loved it. But it wasn't one of these honking things that can carry two round bales of hay that some folks around here drove.

Galen smiled. "It's actually on a trailer already. I keep it on there to make it easier to move in and out of the garage, and it's not very heavy. So I think your girl could tow it over just fine."

I shook my hips in a little happy dance. "You just saved Christmas, Galen."

He blushed and said, "No, no . . . I'm just glad the sleigh is going to get used."

I hugged him tightly, and his blush got deeper against his steel-gray hair. "Want to be an elf?" I asked with a wink.

He held one leg out suggestively and said, "I do look good in tights. But no thanks." He winked back. "I will come by and take a few pics, though, if that's okay."

"More than okay. And your next stack of books is on me. Call it a rental fee."

"Deal," he said and held out his hand to shake. "Come by whenever for the sleigh. I'll text you the address."

"Perfect. Thank you again," I said and squealed. "Santa's Sleigh Ride is a go!"

By Wednesday night, Galen's Instagram promotion, the really amazing window display that Marcus had created, and the sleigh itself had drummed up some big interest in Santa's first night. Fortunately, my parents had offered to host Thanksgiving. Otherwise, Mart, Daniel, and I would probably have had a bag of Bugles, a can of spray cheese, and a bottle of wine for our meal. We were all slammed with holiday prep – Mart at the winery where she worked and Daniel with me at the store, where he was recruited to hang lights and help stock the shelves with the year's hottest titles. Books had always been big sellers during the December holidays, and I wanted to be prepared for even more sales this year.

We had been closed for Thanksgiving, but we opened early on Friday morning with our Black Friday discount of buy three books in one genre get one free. The sale only lasted until ten a.m., and then we went to a straight ten percent off everything until Santa arrived at four p.m.

I'd taken a little inspiration from Galen and arranged an entourage of dogs to "pull" his sleigh for the first customers who arrived, and when a tiny girl with braids and beads in her hair came in the door, she screamed with delight as did her mother. "Doggies!" she said. "Black Santa!" was her mother's joyful sentiment. We were off to a great start.

Soon, the line of folks with their kiddos was out the door, and I realized that I was going to have to serve as the elf and keep the line moving. If I could have, I would have let every child sit for as long – or as short – a time as they wanted, but it soon became clear I was going to have to set a time limit or plan to be here well past midnight. I enlisted Marcus's help, and he drew a quick sign that said, "Santa's legs get tired. Please limit your visits to two requests and three minutes each." That helped some, but of course, some folks also needed to be ushered along with a gentle hand under the elbow.

Mayhem and Mac, our lead "rein-dogs" were holding steady at the front of the lines, but behind them, most of the other pooches, including Cate's restless Schnauzer, Sasquatch, and Mack, were getting restless. So at six, I sent the pups on their way with bags of treats and my hearty thanks, and the sleigh went dogless for the rest of the evening.

Just before nine, we were getting ready to close up, and I was about to fall over from fatigue. Supervising a line of children was exhausting, but it was the persnickety attitudes of some of the parents that were really draining. I simply could *not* with the mother who insisted that her child go back to Santa because she has not requested the right American Girl doll, and the father who felt like his son shouldn't ask for a teddy bear because it was too much of a sissy gift got a stern glare from me and a free copy of *When The Bees Fly Home* to help him and his gorgeous son explore those awful gender stereotypes.

The event had been great, but I was making a little list of things we needed – bottles of water for staff and people in line, a chair for the resident elf, more resident elves – when I saw that the last person in line was a grown man without any children. I kept an eye out, wondering if maybe the child in question was in the restroom, but when he finally made it to Santa, he was still alone. Alone and swaying on his feet.

I gave Marcus a quick wave, and he came over, seeing immediately the issue at hand, and helped me steady our final guest as he reached Santa. I looked at Damien, our Santa, with the obvious question in my eyes, and he took a deep breath before nodding. Then, this thin but very tall white man slumped down into Santa's lap.

"What can Santa do for you this year, er, young man?" Damien boomed in his best Santa voice.

The guy in his lap was now leaning against Damien's chest, and even when Damien jostled around, he didn't move. I groaned, and Marcus and I each took one of the man's arms and pulled him upright off of Damien's lap. But the guy didn't even attempt to hold his own weight. He went right past vertical and slammed into the table in front of him.

For a split second, I continued to think he was drunk until I realized that he hadn't made even a grunt when his nose had smacked into the table top nor when his shoulder had slammed into the floor. "Oh no," I said with horror.

Damien knelt down and put his fingers to the guy's neck. When he wasn't moonlighting as Santa, Damien was a volunteer firefighter and had some medical training. "No pulse," he said. "Call 911." Then, Damien flipped the guy onto his back and started chest compressions as Marcus moved to the man's head, presumably to give him mouth-to-mouth.

For a second, I just stood there, staring, but then I jarred myself into action and dialed.

By the time the ambulance arrived, it was clear this guy wasn't waking up. Someone had died, in Santa's lap, in my bookstore, on the first day of the Christmas season.

2

G iven that it was so late on a Friday night during the holidays, the sheriff, my friend Tucker Mason, didn't keep us long after he arrived to assess the scene. A quick statement from everyone there and we were on our way with a promise to give more information the next morning.

Daniel responded to my SOS text immediately, so he'd arrived at the same time Tuck had. He came right to me, put his arm around my waist, and said, "Good Lord, Harvey. You okay?"

I nodded, unable to speak for fear I would cry. Crying is my emotional response for all sorts of things including terror and rage. So tonight's combo platter of exhaustion, sadness, and confusion was sure to open the floodgates if I opened my mouth. Daniel pulled me close, but he didn't ask me to speak again. He knew.

Normally, I'd walk home. I loved the time to decompress, and the cold air actually helped me relax – I'd always been far more of a winter person than a summer one – but tonight, Daniel insisted on driving me home in my truck, which he drove most of the time, after Marcus, Rocky, and I locked the store. I was glad that Rocky and Marcus had each other, and I was immensely grateful Daniel was there for me, and not just because of the ride. This wasn't the first death in my store.

As we got home, Mart, my roommate and best friend, slammed on her brakes after squealing into the driveway. "Again, Harvey?" she said.

Not her most compassionate greeting, but I couldn't help but echo her question. "Yes, again. This time, though, it wasn't murder." At least I hoped it wasn't.

"That's good then," she said as she unlocked the door and held it open for Daniel and the dogs, who had been in the homemade crates Daniel had crafted for them. "What happened?"

I recounted the scene – the drunk man, the collapse, Marcus doing CPR – as I collapsed onto the couch and gratefully took the glass of wine she handed me. Daniel poured the dogs some food and refreshed their water before sitting down next to me. I leaned my head on his shoulder and wished I could just go to sleep and wake up to find this was all the plot of some book I was reading.

Mart put on the kettle behind us and said, "Wine to calm you. Tea to help you sleep."

I smiled. My friends were good people, which is why I wasn't surprised when the door opened a few minutes later to a steady stream of people I loved, including my friends from San Francisco, Stephen and Walter; Cate and Lucas, Bear and Henri, friends from here; and even my parents. My parents were learning, finally, to take things a little easier here in our sleepy, quiet town. But tonight, they were not exactly exhibiting the calm, relaxed attitudes they'd been cultivating.

"Harvey, what happened?" Mom's voice was just this side of a shriek, and I winced.

This time, Daniel did the honors of telling the story, looking at me carefully to be sure he was getting it right. He told an excellent, brief version of events, and I tried to look like I was sipping, not gulping my wine.

"Sounds like an aneurism," our friend Henri said as she moved her dreadlocks over her shoulder. Henri was a weaver who made these beautiful wall hangings, like the one over our fireplace, and her ever-present artistic look – draping sweaters, wide-legged pants, and adorable tennis shoes – was effortless. Even her dark-brown skin practically glowed, even though I knew – because I'd asked – that her skin-care regimen consisted of Ivory soap morning and night.

Mart nodded. "That's what I was thinking too, or a stroke."

Bear, Henri's husband, rolled his eyes. "The two of you get your medical degrees since I last heard?" Bear was an emergency room doctor, so I was eager to hear what he'd have to say. "I can't even begin to speculate," he said as I gave him my most pointed look.

I sighed.

Cate slid onto the couch next to me and pulled my feet onto her lap and began to massage them. I don't know where she'd picked up this skill or the knowledge that this was the best way in the entire world to relax me, but tonight, I didn't care. I needed a foot massage almost as badly as I needed sleep.

Then, as if by some signal, everyone stopped talking about the man's death and started discussing their holiday plans. I was grateful. We weren't going to bring the man back or erase the fact that he'd died in my store during Christmas by talking about it, and I really wanted to just wind down. I didn't even really listen to what anyone said. I just let the voices of people I loved and who loved me fill the room as I tried not to groan audibly when Cate rubbed the pain out of my arches.

The next thing I knew, I was in bed in my pajamas with a black and white cat on the pillow next to me, and it was morning. I reached over and gave Aslan a scratch. She returned the kindness by deigning to open one eye a sliver and letting out a short purr before settling deeper into her queenly cushion. I looked at the clock: eight-thirty a.m. I stretched and then climbed out of bed with the intention of heading right to the shower and then sprinting to the store to open for our special early hours this holiday weekend. But when I got to the bathroom door, a note read, "I'm opening. Take your time. – Mart."

I smiled and felt my shoulders drop. "Aslan, how does a cup of coffee sound?"

The cat didn't even bother to open an eye this time.

I didn't dawdle long at home, but I did let the hot water run a little longer than I might have just to sooth my aching body. I had slept so hard that I woke up with one of those stiff necks that come from lying in one position too long. The shower helped, but I still popped two ibuprofen and a Tylenol – the pain-med combo that my dentist had prescribed for toothache but had become my standard wonder cure for all pain – while I sipped my coffee and caught up on Galen's Instagram feed.

I took one more minute to scroll the news and social media feeds, but somehow, maybe because of the late hour, the news of the man's death hadn't made it online yet. But I knew, given that this was St. Marin's, it was only a matter of time.

I donned my navy-blue pea coat, wrapped a cashmere scarf that Mart had made around my neck, and leashed up Mayhem for the walk. She had gobbled down her food while I'd swallowed a cinnamon raisin English muffin with honey, and she was ready to go. That dog loved her walks almost as much as she loved her adoring fans at the store.

The walk was perfect and did wonders to limber me up and clear the cobwebs from my mind. The air was crisp and the sky the perfect blue of late autumn. By the time I neared the store, the only question I had was about who had gotten me into bed last night. I prayed it was Mart. Daniel and I were not moving fast physically, although we had gotten engaged a few weeks ago, and I hated the thought that the first glimpse he'd have of his fiancé in her underwear would include my Loony Toons granny panties.

I didn't have long to wait to find out the great mystery because Mart texted and said, "All set at the store. Marcus and Rocky are on it. BTW, Tweety always was my favorite."

I guffawed and startled a tiny woman just entering the store. Then, I let out a long sigh of relief. "Mine, too," I texted back. "Obviously."

I was glad Mart had clarified for me because when Daniel came in a few minutes later, I was glad to be able to look him in the face without blushing. Well, without blushing too much. He still made me a little weak in the knees.

"Saw Tuck on my way in this morning. He asked me to meet him here at ten. I think he wants to talk to all of you." He looked from me to Marcus at the register and over to Rocky in the café. "I have a suspicion that I'm about to finally learn how to run your cash register."

As if on cue, Tuck walked in the front door and, with a nod, signaled to Rocky, Marcus, and me that our presence was requested in the back room. Yet again, I was grateful for the table and the chairs I'd added to our make-shift break room, but my sincere appreciation of those items dulled to the enthusiasm that sparked in me when I saw that Rocky was bringing a full carafe of coffee and a plate of cinnamon scones.

I took the stack of recyclable cups from under her arm and took the opportunity to give her a quick squeeze of thanks before we pushed open the stockroom door and saw the dark circles under Tuck's eyes. "Did you get any sleep?" I asked as I sat down.

He shook his head. "No, and Lu had me up at three yesterday morning to get to the big sales in Baltimore. After this, I am going home and not waking up until Monday."

I poured him a huge cup of coffee and saw that Rocky had wisely brought the dark roast. I hesitated in my temptation to add a big dose from the sugar bottle on the table, but I knew Tuck preferred his coffee black. Even the thought made my lips pucker.

Everyone got their coffee prepped and a scone in hand, and then Tuck had us review the events of the night before – together – unlike last night when he'd interviewed each of us separately. We walked him through the evening, the dogs, the children we could remember, and then finally the last visitor for Santa. At this point, he slowed us down and asked us to describe the guy's behavior very specifically.

All of us had seen him come in. At first, he had seemed tipsy, and I definitely had smelled beer on his breath. I realized that's why I thought he sat with Damien, that he was drunk.

"He wasn't drunk, was he?" I asked right in the middle of Rocky's description of the man. "Oh, sorry, Rocky." I shrugged and tried to look apologetic.

"What?!" Marcus said and then looked at Tuck. "He wasn't drunk?"

"Actually, no. He had been drinking, but his blood alcohol level wasn't high enough for him to show visible symptoms." Tuck said before he took a long sip of his very hot coffee without even a wince. "We're waiting for the autopsy, but it looks like he was drugged. The ME expects it was an insulin overdose."

My eyes went very wide. "Is that even a thing?"

"Apparently, yes. And it mimics the symptoms of intoxication – stumbling, slurred speech, glassy eyes." Tuck looked at Rocky. "Is that what you saw?"

Rocky nodded. "Pretty much." She turned to me. "How did you know?"

"Just something about the way he talked when he got up from Damien's lap. It was like his mouth wasn't really working. I mean like *really* not working." I shrugged. "I don't really know how to describe it."

Marcus nodded. "I think I know what you mean. It was not quite right for a guy who'd had too much to drink."

"Exactly. He seemed too out of it *and* too coherent for him to be totally drunk." I paused and thought about the few times I'd had too much to drink and the people I knew who really drank to excess. This guy hadn't seemed like them somehow. "I guess it seems like if he had drunk enough to stumble like that and slur so badly, he wouldn't have actually been able to walk to the store. Plus, his words were in the wrong order, I think."

"That's right," Rocky said as she sat forward in her chair. "Now that you mention it, I remember thinking he sounded like the toddlers at the daycare where my sister works. They know words, but not rules for using them. So the words are in the wrong order or not quite right."

"Yeah," Marcus sighed. "He kept saying, 'Best everyone help.'"

Tuck was jotting down everything we were saying, and I was getting more and more anxious the more he wrote.

"You don't think this was an accident, do you, Tuck?" The knot in my throat made it hard for me to swallow.

He sighed and put his pen down. "No. We think someone dosed him. On purpose."

I looked from Rocky to Marcus and back to Tuck. "He was murdered," I whispered.

"It appears that way, Harvey. I'm sorry. I know this isn't the kick-off to your Christmas season that you wanted." The sheriff stood and put his baseball cap back on his head. "I'll let you know anything relevant, and of course, if any of you think of anything else . . ."

Marcus stood and shook the sheriff's hand. "We know where to find you."

Rocky slid her chair over next to me as Marcus and the sheriff walked out. "You okay?" she said.

I put my cheek on the table and thought about how I'd

loved those infrequent naps you got in elementary school, about how the cool desktop had felt so great for a few minutes. I wanted one of those naps now, and when I woke up, I was hoping it would be fifth grade again. Even the likes of my childhood nemesis David McElroy on the kickball field wouldn't be as daunting as a murder in my store at Christmas.

3

———

Eventually, Rocky lured me out of the back room with the promise of a double-shot latte and one of her mom's cinnamon rolls, and I peeled myself off the table and made it to the register just in time to see Daniel hand-sell a beautiful copy of *The Quilts of Gee's Bend* that Cate had talked me into adding to my art book collection, despite the high cover price. The man buying it did not look like a quilter, but he did look like an art collector, which made sense since those gorgeous quilts were works of historical art. Henri admired the quilters of Gee's Bend and had even spent some time with them to see what she might incorporate in her weavings from their patterns. I was glad the book had found a new home with someone who would appreciate it. I was also glad for the nice mark-up. It might make up for some of the inevitable lost sales that would come once word got out that a murder victim had succumbed while telling Santa all he wanted for Christmas.

Even the thought of murder made me groan, but I tried to simply put my head down and get to work. Saturday was usually our busiest day of the week, and with the holidays coming, I was hoping to see our revenues climb back up to the range they'd been in the high tourist season of summer. I just couldn't see that happening what with the death in Santa's lap and all . . .

But of course, I underestimated the human fascination with all things macabre, and by noon, the shop was full, Rocky had pulled out the extra coffee carafes, and I had fielded about a million questions about when The Slaying Santa would be in again. I had a deep fondness for word play, but this nickname was not my favorite.

Damien, however, the Santa in question, loved it, and even signed a few autographs when he came in for his afternoon session. "Harvey, thank you. I've already gotten two other Santa gigs because of the press around this one."

I stared at him for a very long moment before I actually managed to say, "People want to hire you *because* someone died on you."

He blushed a little. "Well, they are Christmas haunted houses so . . ."

"Wait, what?! There's such a thing as a Christmas haunted house?" I stared again. The wonders never cease. I tried to put a smile on my face and said, "Seriously, though, are you okay, Damien? I mean that was a big deal."

His face grew serious. "Yeah, I am. I talked to my counselor this morning, made sure I had some things in place in case I started to feel weirded out. Sad about the guy, though. Know anything about him?"

"Not much." I told him the little bit the sheriff had told us, and the color faded from Damien's face.

"Oh man, I definitely need to take a minute and visualize my safe place. I'm glad I talked to my therapist." He headed toward the back room, white beard in tow, and I hoped he'd find his meditation helpful.

When I got stressed, I thought about this bench that overlooked the Golden Gate – the water, not the bridge – in San Francisco. I'd picture the place, try to smell the eucalyptus, watch the pelicans soar by. I always felt better, more grounded when I did, so I was glad that Damien had something like that to use, too. Death was always hard, but violent death . . . let's just say I had gone to my safe space a lot in my head this morning while the sheriff asked us questions.

While Damien prepared himself for the literal throngs of people waiting to see him, I decided to up the cheer in the store a notch and popped in the *Trolls Holiday* album. The kids loved it, and I had yet to meet an adult who could withstand the pep of Justin Timberlake singing "Love Train."

Within seconds, heads were bobbing, and I could just feel the Christmas spirit starting to loosen itself from the dark corners of the store. We'd have enough to contend with in the coming days. Right now, I just wanted to enjoy my peppermint latte and dance a little among the books. From what I could see, I wasn't alone. People were shimmying all over the store, and it was wonderful.

I spent the next few hours making small displays of holiday books all around the store. My favorite was a table full of picture books that my mother had in her picture book collection including *The Littlest Angel* by Charles Tazewell. I loved that story of a tiny angel who didn't think he had much to offer but learns, as we all do, that who is he is enough of a gift. I had to resist reading it as soon as I put it out.

Business was swift, and Damien had a long line again. I tried to not let it bother me too much that a fair number of his "guests" were adults clearly seeking a little macabre thrill. Damien handled them deftly by pulling up a chair next to him, listening to whatever they said. As I passed by once, I heard a woman ask for a new husband for Christmas and a later young man say that he felt weird but really just wanted to see the guy who had held a dead body. Damien escorted that young man to the door himself and then took a break. On his way to the back room, he asked me to give Tuck a ring and give him that guy's description. I had already picked up my phone to do the same. That dude gave me the willies.

Typically, I'd head home in the later afternoon and let Marcus take over closing duties, but given the season and the events of yesterday, I decided to stay on and just order in for dinner. When I called Tuck about the creepster with Santa, he mentioned that his wife Lu's food truck was just up the street, and I took a quick break to slip up there and get a couple of her amazing carnitas tacos. She made the best food in town, hands down, and I think she knew that. But she never said anything because she was humble and also because she was wise. No reason to stoke the ire of local restaurant owner, Max Davies. That man was enough of a pain as it was. The guy had a crush on me, and I really, really didn't want to see him tonight. So I went so far as to bend low at the waist when I passed his restaurant's windows. Hopefully, I looked like a small, navy-blue bear hunching by on the sidewalk.

But not even having to hide from Max was going to deter me from enjoying dinner. It had taken a lot of willpower not to start chowing down before I got to the store. I resisted, and Lu's tacos in hand, I slipped into a corner of the café to eat and sip my decaf peppermint latte – no caffeine after three if I wanted to sleep that night. Near me, three women in hospital scrubs were enjoying some of Rocky's lattes themselves. I could hear them admiring her steamed milk Christmas trees and ornaments. Apparently, she'd also branched into the other holidays, which I loved, because one woman was marveling at her menorah.

I scarfed down my dinner and was just washing up in the small sink behind Rocky's counter when Sheriff Tucker came in and gave me the old "into the back" nod. I sighed but then decided I still wanted to keep the holiday spirit and decided to skip into the back room. A middle-aged woman skipping is a sight that brings one of two reactions: joyous giggles or intense eye rolls. I got a fair share of both, but I think the giggles took it ... and so a little embarrassment on my part was worth it.

Tuck wasn't laughing when I sat down beside him, though. In fact, he looked downright furious. So much so, that I pushed my chair back just a bit so as to give the anger a little more space in the room. It didn't look like Tuck was ready to talk yet, so I looked around the room for something to keep me busy. Normally, I'd do a jigsaw puzzle on my phone or read a book or something, but I'd left my phone at the counter, and I didn't think rifling through the boxes of books for a new title was appropriate at the moment. So I settled for counting how many doorknobs were in the room. It was a short count – four to be exact – but it gave Tuck a chance to collect himself without me pressuring him to talk.

When I swung my eyes back to him, he was staring at his hands, and now his expression had turned to sorrow. "What is it, Tuck?" I asked as I leaned forward across the table.

"I just learned that our victim was a nurse at the hospital."

I sat back with a thud. "Man. Do you know his name?"

"Rupert Bixley, but everybody called him 'Rope." Tuck sighed.

I stifled a giggle and cleared my throat before speaking. "Rope?" The way Southern people give each other nicknames always cracks me up, and that's saying something because I'm a woman who goes by Harvey.

"Guess he got it in high school gym class—"

I interrupted, "Because he could do that freakish thing of climbing the rope to the gym ceiling?"

"Exactly. That plus Rupert . . ." Tuck's face looked a little less tense, but something else was on his mind. Anyone being killed was tragic, and the death of someone who had dedicated their lives to helping others added a level of distress. But this reaction from the sheriff seemed to be about something more.

"Okay, but what aren't you telling me?" For a second, I thought about adding, "And why are you telling me anything since you tell me to butt out of your investigations all the time?" but I didn't want to scare him off. I had an undying – no pun intended – fascination with murder investigations, and if Tuck was going to let me behind the scenes, I wasn't about to miss this chance.

He met my eyes for the first time. "I have no evidence, Harvey, and I'm mostly just here because I needed to talk this through with someone. Lu's at the truck, and I don't want my deputies having this information yet. I need someone with a good head who can keep things quiet while I investigate. I saw you in the café, and so, well, here I am." He put a hand on my arm. "But seriously, Harvey, nothing I say here can go behind this room, not even to Daniel or Mart, okay?'

I nodded, sincerely, and hoped I was better at keeping a secret this time than I had been in the past. "What's going on?"

"I have reason to believe that Bixley was an angel of mercy."

Images of convents and those creepy angels from *Doctor Who* flashed through my mind until something snagged, and I said, "The people who kill patients?"

He nodded. "Yes. They start out thinking they're helping people who are suffering too much, but then, sometimes – and that looks like the case with Bixley – they can't stop and kill healthy people, too."

I took a long, deep breath. "Can you tell me what makes you think this is a possibility?"

"A couple of the nurses I talked to hinted at it. No one wanted to say anything directly, but they suggested I look into a few recent deaths." He ran his hands over his shaved head. "When I did, well, I need to have a medical professional look at what I found, but ten people died on his shift for reasons that don't make sense."

"How do ten people die for no reason and no one asks questions?" I could feel my anger rising.

"Most of them were sick, really sick – cancer mostly – so I guess people thought that it was natural. Only two of them had autopsies." He took his notebook out of his breast pocket. "Now that I say that, that's weird isn't it?"

I shrugged. "I don't really know. If they were dying already, maybe the family didn't want or think they needed to know the literal cause. Maybe cancer was enough reason?"

"That makes sense, but what I don't get is why no one at the hospital looked into it." His jaw clenched as he leaned back in his chair. "Surely someone must have noticed."

"Sounds like those two nurses did. Maybe they just didn't know what to do about it?" I'd been in plenty of situations like that, where I knew there was a problem but had no idea how to address it. Still, this was people's lives we were talking about. Plus, these things were happening at a hospital. I could see Tuck's point. "You're right, though, something is off."

He stood up and slid his baseball cap back on his head. "Thanks, Harvey. You're a good listener." As he put his hand on doorknob #1 that went out into the shop, he looked back. "Not a word, though, okay?"

I nodded. And then I prayed I could keep my big mouth shut.

4

My prayers were answered, albeit a little unexpectedly, when all my friends showed up at the store for one of our now pretty regular impromptu picnics. This time, though, it was Daniel – not Cate and Lucas – who brought the main course – a big aluminum foil pan of North Carolina-style pork barbecue. I could smell the tang of vinegar in the air as he set the pan on the counter by the register and immediately scanned everyone else's hands to be sure that the other three essentials – cole slaw, hamburger buns, and hot pepper vinegar – were on their way. I was not disappointed. Woody, a first-timer for our bookstore gathering, carried a mason jar of what looked like pickled peppers, and behind him, Henri and Bear had bags of potato buns and a bowl of cole slaw. Lucas traipsed in soon after with a platter of his delectable cupcakes, and Marcus pulled out two gallons of sweet (but decaf) iced tea from behind the counter. Even Pickle brought a contribution, a container of St. Marin's finest potato salad which was, much to most tourists' surprise, made at the local gas station.

By the time I got out the plates, cups, napkins, and forks I'd begun buying in bulk and storing in the back room, Lu and Tuck had joined the group, as had Mart with her love-sick beau, Symeon. Fortunately for Mart, she was as head over heels for him as he for her, or it would have been annoying how he doted on her. It annoyed me a bit in fact, just because I missed my best friend and roomie, but I remembered my rule about new relationships – everyone gets four months to forget all their friends without remorse before people can stop complaining about their PDA and incessant relating of every cute thing about their new partner. Mart and Symeon were just about at that point, but given that we were in the holiday season, I was willing to extend their grace period.

I had just made myself not one but two barbecue sand-wiches with lots of hot pepper vinegar and coleslaw on the side – the heathens who marred that beautiful pork with slaw on the sandwich never made sense to me – when Stephen and Walter arrived with a thermos of something that smelled amaz-ing. "Gentlemen, what did you bring?"

Stephen grinned. "I've been trying my hand at hot toddies and thought I might beg for some taste testers."

"Please. I cannot drink one more sip of cardamom," Walter said as he rolled his eyes at his husband.

"Beg your pardon. This one has cinnamon." He grinned and held up the thermos.

Rocky jogged back to the café and came over with to-go cups so that all of us could taste "St. Stephen's Hot Chocolate," and before long the thermos was empty, and our bellies were full of good food and warm chocolate and coconut. "I didn't even know they made coconut liqueur," Daniel said as he slid to a fully reclined position against the arm of the wing-back chair I'd scored by being first in the food line.

"I didn't either, but it's good, huh?" Stephen said without a hint of false modesty. "I'm trying to figure out what holiday-esque drink involves banana for my next experiment."

I shuddered. If there was one flavor I did not like, it was fake banana. Left a film on my tongue that I couldn't shake for hours. But I kept my mouth shut because, clearly, this new hobby was giving my friend joy.

Cate scooted her matching wingback over closer to mine as everyone else continued to talk about their favorite holiday drinks. I clinked my paper cup against hers and raised an eyebrow. "What's up, woman?"

"Angel of mercy, I hear."

My eyes darted over to Tuck, but he was thoroughly engrossed in conversation with Lucas. "Where did you hear that?" I asked, hoping I sounded more unaware than I was.

"I knew you'd already heard," Cate laughed as I realized that I hadn't asked the logical question: "What are you talking about?"

I sighed. "Yes, I heard. Who did you hear from?"

"Oh, two of the janitors from the hospital come clean the co-op after they finish their night shift. They were talking about it while they mopped." Cate was the owner and manager of our local art co-op and a talented photographer herself. "Those poor people. I mean, I'm pretty sure that I'd be trying to find a way to end my pain if I was suffering at the end, but I'd want that to be my decision, not someone else's, you know?"

I did know. It's all I'd been thinking about since Tuck had stopped by. I wasn't sure what I thought about assisted suicide, but I definitely knew what I thought about homicide. And while I didn't think Bixley had gotten what he deserved, especially since we weren't sure he had committed any crimes, I could understand why someone might revenge if they thought he had killed a person they loved. "It's all just horrible."

"What's horrible?" Daniel asked into the now-quiet room. "You okay?"

Again, I looked at Tuck, and he rolled his eyes. "It's okay, Harvey. The rumor is out. You can talk."

I let out a burst of air and said, "Thank God. I hate secrets."

"It's been two hours, Harvey. Not even," Tuck said.

"The longest two hours of my life," I said with intentional hyperbole as I glanced at Mart.

She shrugged. "Care to clue the rest of us in on what you've had to keep quiet about for an excruciating one hundred and twenty minutes?"

I looked at Tuck again and he made a little shooing motion with his hand, like he needed to push me onto stage. "Apparently, the man who died here last night was an angel of mercy."

Henri gasped. "You mean one of those people who kill dying people?" The color washed out of her face. "I thought that was only a TV thing."

"Wait, what?!" Pickle said. "I'm confused. Someone kills people who are dying anyway."

Tuck cleared his throat and explained that for angels of mercy, they get a thrill from feeling like a hero, even though they're a murderer. "They're serial killers, just not sensational ones," he said as Lu squeezed his forearm. "It's horrible. Worse than even the really sick killers, in my opinion, because these people have usually sworn an oath to do no harm and yet they take the privilege that oath provides and use it to kill." His voice was quivery, and Lu pulled him close.

"Despicable," Lucas said with a glance at Cate. "When my sister was dying of ALS, a lot of people offered ways to help her end her suffering. She considered some of them, and," he swallowed hard, "I often hoped she'd do something because it was so awful to watch her die that way. But it was her decision to make, not someone else's."

I sighed. "I'm so sorry, Lucas, and you're right. It was her decision."

The bookshop got very quiet for few minutes, but finally, Marcus spoke. "If that's true, this dude, he was a monster – but I still believe that even monsters deserve justice, not murder."

A small murmur of affirmation went through the room as we all turned toward Tuck. "Anything you need, Sheriff?" Daniel asked.

Tuck smiled a tiny grin. "Well, now that you mention it, I do need someone to go undercover."

At the exact same moment, Mart and Daniel grabbed my arms and held them down, which was an annoying reaction on their part, albeit justified since my hand was already on the rise when they got hold of me.

"Volunteer for what?" Bear asked. As a doctor in the ER at the hospital, he must be having a particularly hard time with this news, but his face was placid.

"I suspect Bixley wasn't working alone, and I need someone to play a dying patient," Tuck said tentatively.

Mart's and Daniel's grips on my arms tightened, and before I could wrench free, Cate said, "I'll do it."

Lucas looked as his wife and said, "Are you sure?"

Cate nodded, her black hair bouncing against her porcelain skin. "What do I need to do?"

She, Lucas, Tuck and Lu moved to a café table to strategize, and the rest of us sat in a heavy silence on the floor of the bookstore. Absentmindedly, I scooped all the frosting off the remaining three of Lucas's cupcakes and then stared in horror at the naked cake beneath.

Daniel handed me a napkin as he shoved an entire chocolate cupcake in his mouth. "Thank you. The frosting was too much for me tonight."

I leaned over and kissed his cake-filled mouth. "You are too sweet."

"Hey, if all I need to do to get a kiss is eat some cake, I'll buy a dozen of Lucas's goods every day," he said as tiny pieces of chocolate fell from his mouth.

"That won't be necessary." I smiled at him, but I still felt uneasy, helpless. I needed to do something.

I stood up and stretched and then began to pace the store. Books – as artifacts, as art, and as things to read – always gave me sustenance, and so walking around the store, *my* store, calmed me and helped me think. I was just on my second pass through the shelves when I stopped short in the "Death and Dying" shelf of the Psychology Section. There, I had carefully curated a few dozen books on the subject, trying to represent the various ways people might find what they needed to prepare or to grieve. I ran my fingers along the spine of *The Year of Magical Thinking* by Joan Didion and then I remembered listening to Paul Kalanithi's *When Breath Becomes Air* on one of the drives I took along the backroads of the Eastern Shore on my rare days off. His wisdom about death, his peace with his own death gave me an idea.

I marched back to my friends and said, "I have an idea. Let's do a fundraiser."

Marcus handed Rocky a five-dollar bill and said, "How did you know?"

"If there's one thing that Harvey does just as well as she sells books, it's raise money," Rocky said with a wink at me. "Who are we raising money for this time, boss lady?"

I looked over at Lucas and thought about his sister. "Hospice. Let's raise money for our local hospice."

Bear grinned and stood. "I like this idea, Harvey. I like it a lot. There aren't many better organizations than hospice. Let me help you organize this one?"

I grinned at my friend and took his dark brown hand in my white one. "You lead, and I'll follow. Want to meet tomorrow and make a plan?"

Bear nodded. "Thank you, Harvey."

I squeezed his fingers and nodded. Yep, this situation was hard for him. I looked down at Henri, and she let out a long breath and then smiled at me.

"It's a date, then," I said as I began to gather up the trash.

"What's a date?" Cate asked as she and Lucas came back over to join us.

"You'll be shocked to hear," Woody said as he pried himself out of a super comfy chair and a half, "that Harvey is planning another fundraiser, this one for hospice."

I glanced at Lucas and saw tears pool in his eyes before he looked away.

"Oh, that's wonderful," Cate said. "You know I'm in."

"Me, too," said Mart with Symeon echoing her immediately. And around the room, everyone offered to help. I felt tears prick my own eyes at the joy of my friends.

"Okay, let Bear and me get the plan in place, and then we'll loop you all in. Sound good?"

Everyone nodded and then began to gather their dishes and return the chairs to their respective places in the store. As I bent to pick up the last of the hot chocolate cups, Tuck stepped beside me and said, "This is a good idea, Harvey. People are really upset about this situation. It'll help them to have something else to focus on."

I smiled and let myself feel happy for just a moment in this weird, hard weekend. Then, I walked all my friends to the door, set the alarm, and took Daniel's arm as we closed the shop for the night.

IT WAS A LOVELY, crisp evening, and while I was bone-tired, I didn't feel like going home yet. And Mayhem and Taco were apparently invigorated by the cold air and from an entire day of sleeping because they were adamant about sniffing every single tree, twig, and lamppost in sight. Daniel and I decided to meander the streets of downtown, and as we walked, I started to brainstorm ideas. "What if we brought in experts to talk about death and grief and let them have a forum in the store? Then, we could take donations for hospice at that event but also provide some resources for people who needed them."

Daniel had been with me long enough to know that I didn't really need to have him say anything when I got on these jags of creative talk. His listening ear and calm presence were more than enough to spur me on.

"When Mart's mom was sick, hospice came regularly to visit with her mom, but they also sent a chaplain to meet with Mart and her dad and help them with what the dying process would look like." I remembered that in the last few weeks of her life, Mrs. Weston had become skeletal. She hadn't looked like herself at all, and most days, she simply slept. Mart had moved home to Iowa from San Francisco to help her dad when it looked like the end was near, and she'd gotten training from hospice about how to lift her mother to help change her bed linens and about how to help keep her comfortable.

I leaned my head against Daniel's shoulder as we walked. "I remember that Mart said the hospice nurses warned her that her mother would rally just before the end and that while this was a moment to cherish, it did not mean she was improving, but just the opposite. Mart said that was the most helpful piece of information she ever received because when her mom did, indeed, rally, she was able to wheel her outside and let her enjoy the sunshine, to have a last conversation with her, and then to prepare for her death." I felt tears sliding down my face as I thought about how devastated Mart had been when her mom died, but she had also been ready, or as ready as someone can be.

"Mart has always said that hospice helped her mom, but it saved her." I paused and filled my lungs with the cold night air. "I'd like to dedicate this fundraiser to Mrs. Weston, to honor her and Mart."

Daniel put his hand on my cheek and kissed me. "I think that's a beautiful idea, Harvey. A beautiful idea."

We had made our way back to Main Street, and, given the late hour, only a few people were out and about, mostly leaving Chez Cuisine, Max's restaurant. One young woman with skin the color of burnished cedar was speaking loudly to the other women in her group. "I can't even believe it. Bixley. I mean he was a royal jerk, but a killer? I did not see that coming. Sounds like he got what he deserved."

Just then, she caught sight of Daniel and me and stopped short. I smiled at her, trying to put her at ease, but she glowered back at me.

I leaned into Daniel and feigned interest in whatever Mayhem was sniffing now as we made our way past. That woman's stare made my skin prickle.

5

The next afternoon at three, Henri and Bear showed up at the café for our fundraising meeting, and they had prepared.

"I made a couple of calls this morning, and while I haven't committed to anything, I wonder how you'd feel about having John Green come and speak about his experience of writing *The Fault In Our Stars* and his own views on death and dying," Bear said as nonchalantly as if he'd just asked me if I liked the old weather.

I stared at my friend for a long moment before I could speak. "John Green? The author John Green? Maybe the most popular young adult author in the country, John Green?" I looked at Henri, and she nodded with a sly grin as she twisted one of her dreadlocks around and around her finger.

"I met him a few years back through work." I knew better than to ask for more details. Bear was beyond respectful of patient privacy. "We've stayed in touch, and he said he'll be in DC in a couple of weeks and could fit in a reading and conversation here for such a good cause."

I blinked several times and tried to form sentences. "You're telling me – Are you saying – What?!"

Henri took my hand. "Just say yes, Harvey."

"Yes, yes. One hundred million times yes. When?"

"Two weeks from today," Bear said.

My stomach lurched a bit. I was going to have two weeks to pull off the biggest event of my life with an author I admired immensely. I started to panic, but Henri spoke slowly and softly. "You don't have to do much, Harvey. John's publicity team will do the bulk of the work, and really, the event will sell itself."

"Which brings up another thing we need to discuss," Bear said as a surge of panic flushed my body.

"Where in the world are we going to have this? We can't do it here."

Henri stood up, walked over, and began giving me a shoulder rub. "Relax, Harvey. We have options." Her hands were so strong from weaving, I presumed, and I immediately began to relax.

"Okay, what options? I'd like to have it here in town if we could, give St. Marin's a little boost in the off-season." Our adorable town was kept financially alive because of the water-based tourists who came from April to October. The winter months were often lean for business owners.

"Agreed," Bear said. "Two options – we could do it at the maritime museum auditorium. It holds a couple of hundred people. Or we could use the high school gym, which will seat considerably more and—"

"And," I couldn't stop myself from interrupting, "would be ideal both because of the capacity and because Green writes YA novels?"

"Precisely," Bear said with a smile. "You took the words right out of my mouth." He winked at me, and I tried to shrug my shoulders but found Henri's massage held them down.

"Sorry, Bear. I'm just excited. This is a huge deal." I tried to lean forward to hug him, but Henri's kneading fingers, once again, kept me in my seat. "Thank you. Really."

Bear leaned back in his chair. "Well, there is something you can do for me?"

"Anything," I said, this time tapping Henri's right hand and then breaking free to lean closer to her husband. "What do you need?"

"I need you to keep me in the loop about the investigation."

My stomach plummeted again. "Bear!" I could hear the whine in my voice. This was the last thing I wanted to do. Okay, it was the thing I most wanted to do AND the last thing I wanted to do. Daniel and Mart would kill me if I got involved.

"I know, Harvey. It's a big ask, and I'll still help you with the fundraiser, even if you say no, but this hits very close to home, you know?"

I did know. Bear took his work as a physician very seriously. He served on the hospital board, and he took a trip every summer to provide medical care in Haiti. I couldn't imagine how it must feel to have someone use your profession in such an awful way. I was, once again, glad I ran a bookstore. At least people didn't kill people over books. At least I hoped they didn't.

I took a deep breath. "I can't make any promises, but I will let you know what I learn when I learn it, okay?"

He smiled and patted my hand. "Deal. Now, let's get started with the nitty gritty of this event, shall we?"

Henri took at seat and pulled out her calendar. I set mine beside hers, and we delved into what we needed in terms of ticket sales, publicity, etc. By the time we had pinned down all the things we could think of, it was starting to get dark, and I needed to close up the shop.

I was just moving toward the first customers to give them the fifteen-minute warning, when the bell over the front door rang. I groaned inwardly because this was my least favorite thing about retail work – the people who came in at the last minute. Once in a while, they knew exactly what they wanted, grabbed it, and checked out. But usually, they were the epitome of browsers. They hadn't looked at the store's hours as they came in, and they planned to sit and look at every astrology book I had for the entire night.

I shot Rocky a look as I passed in front of the café, and she shook her head a little. Then, I saw her grab the coffee carafes off the bar and turn off the light in the pastry case. *Good woman*, I thought. At least this person wouldn't be able to sip an espresso while they lingered.

The next ten minutes passed quickly as I went to the few remaining customers and asked them to head to the register to make their final purchases. Most nights, this was a pleasant task, a chance to talk with my shoppers personally, but tonight, I was exhausted and was just wishing for a PA system where I could make one announcement and get on with the other closing duties.

I rounded the final shelf of my sweep and nearly stepped on a woman sitting on the floor. "I'm so sorry," I said. "I didn't see you there."

She looked up at me, and I recognized her as the woman who had been talking about Bixley the night before. Tonight, though, she seemed even more angry than when she caught me staring the previous evening. At first, I thought it was because I'd never crushed her with my yarn-covered Dansko, but then she spoke. "Oh, it's you."

Previously, when people described someone as saying their name with venom, I always get a little confused. What exactly does snake poison sound like? I'd think. Tonight, I learned the answer to my question. This woman was ready to strike, and I took a step back.

"Um, yeah, it's me. I'm Harvey Beckett. This is my shop. And you are?"

"Cynthia Delilah." She stood gracefully from the floor and rounded on me. "You need to stop this nonsense."

I stared down at her beautifully manicured hand and thought about deflecting her very intense anger with a comment about her choice of polish color. I thought about it, that is, until I looked into her face again and saw she was probably going to crack a tooth if she clenched her jaw any harder. I took another step back and said, my voice cracking, "I'm so sorry. I have no idea what you're talking about."

She stepped toward me, and I instinctively moved back again only to find that the shelf of Western novels stood in my way. "You. You and that sheriff. You think you have this all figured out. But you have no idea. Bixley was scum, but this idea that someone was working with him—"

Here, my confusion and alarm got the better of me, and I interrupted. "Where did you hear that?" I mean, it was true, but Tuck had only mentioned that to me in the break room the day before. The sheriff was not loose-lipped about cases, so I was thoroughly confused.

"That doesn't matter, now does it." Cynthia was so close that I could see the porcelain fillings in her back molars. "It's a ridiculous idea. Bixley was a monster, but that doesn't mean anyone else is. So *back off.*" She jabbed her immaculate finger into my chest and then spun on her heel and walked away, a copy of *The Diving Bell and the Butterfly* under her arm.

I fumed after her to tell her that she had no right to talk to me and that she owed me twelve dollars for the book, but by the time I stepped out onto the street, she was gone. I stood there in the cold air and let it calm me, and then I walked back in and called Tuck. He needed to hear about the lady who doth protest too much.

· · ·

MY CONVERSATION with Tuck was short and to the point. He said he'd look into it, and I felt good having passed along the information. *Now, I can let it go,* I thought, but of course, I couldn't. I cleaned up the store and helped Rocky wipe down the café tables. We locked up together, and Mayhem and I escorted her to her car.

Then, I decided to take another walk. Walking always helped me think, and I wasn't eager to go home to the empty house just yet. Mart was away on business until tomorrow, and while Aslan, my cat, would surely punish me for not coming home and letting her ignore me, I needed to let the anger I'd felt from that confrontation wander out of me. Plus, there was something niggling at me about the book Cynthia had stolen.

Mayhem was calmer tonight, so our pace was leisurely. I wandered down the other side of Main Street, peeking at the cute clothes in the new vintage and consignment shop that had just opened. I peeked in to Elle's farm shop to be sure she still had a couple of butternut squashes so that I could fix my hankering for butternut squash soup. I gazed at the necklaces in the jewelry store and pondered, not for the first time, why I didn't really care about diamonds or fancy bracelets when, apparently, so many women did.

As I made my way back to my store and on toward home, I thought about Cynthia. The book she'd stolen was one that had been immensely popular about fifteen years earlier when it first came out. It told the story of a man who became trapped in his own body after a stroke. It didn't seem coincidental that Cynthia had been looking at a book about someone who, some would argue, was suffering tremendously in his current physical state, someone who might become the victim of an angel of mercy, perhaps.

I could feel myself getting to some sort of insight about that when an arm slid across my shoulders, and I looked over into the face of Max Davies. It was only then that I realized I had been staring into his restaurant while I was lost in thought, and I wanted to kick myself for my own lack of self-awareness. "Hello, mon amour," he whispered almost directly into my ear.

I jumped back and pushed him at the same time. Then, I stepped off the curb and turned my ankle. Badly. I felt tears spring to my eyes, and I sat down. Mayhem, thank goodness, pushed between me and Max and sat against me. *Good dog.*

"Oh darling, are you hurt?" Max asked as he leaned down directly into my face.

I was not in the mood for anyone, but especially not Max, to get in my face again tonight, so I snapped, "I am not your darling. Now get out of my face." I pushed hard against the curb and tried to stand in as big a posture as I could manage, but my ankle gave way beneath me. The worst part of that was that for a split second I was glad Max caught me.

That second was very short, though, because Max said, "Oh, my clumsy woman, let me carry you inside." Then, he bent and tried to sweep my feet out from under me, bringing us both crashing to the pavement and knocking my temple against the curb.

I groaned and forced myself to sit again. Out of reflex, I looked to see if Max was okay and found that I had broken his fall. I expected he had let me drop to protect himself, but my head was throbbing too much to say anything. "Get away from me, Max." I pulled my phone out of my back pocket and dialed.

"Hi. It's me. I'm okay, but I could use a ride home. I'm in front of Chez Cuisine."

6

Thank goodness Daniel's apartment was just a block away because he was there in a matter of moments. Not soon enough, though, to keep Max from spreading out a cloth napkin on the sidewalk beside me and then sitting down far too close. "How do you make it through the day with such a lack of grace?" he said with a smile.

This was, of course, Max's idea of a friendly joke, but given that I had, at least, a terrible sprain to my ankle and what was quickly becoming a massive goose egg on my head, I was not in the mood to even try to humor him. I'm not usually in that mood, but tonight, less so.

I glowered. I'm pretty sure I looked ridiculous, but I'm certain I didn't look amused because Max slid a few inches away from me and tried to look embarrassed. He didn't succeed, but he tried.

A moment later, Daniel pulled up in my truck, a truck he bought me but that he really drove most of the time. He took one look at me and marched over to Max. "Thank you for keeping Harvey company, Max. I'll take over from here." Daniel's voice sounded much deeper than his usual medium

timbre, and I smiled a little at my not-very-macho guy trying to
seem tough.

Max took the hint – or the escape maybe – and said good
night. Then, Daniel reached down a hand and pulled me to my
feet . . . well to my foot. There was no way I was putting weight
on my sprained ankle again. Nope. With my arm around
Daniel's shoulders, I hopped to the truck and levered myself in.
Daniel got Meander into her custom kennel in the bed, and I
heard Taco yip a word of greeting. While Daniel drove to my
house, I relayed the events of the evening.

I downplayed the Cynthia part of the story because I was
still fuming over Max's bravado and clumsiness, and Daniel
gladly obliged by offering to plant rats in his kitchen or stand
outside with a sandwich board about Armageddon. By the time
he has listed all the ways he could exact our revenge on Max
Davies, I was crying from laughter and had almost forgotten
about the timpani-sized pounding going on in my head.

When we got to my house, Daniel grabbed a dolly that Mart
had left parked by the front walk after she'd brought us a case
of her winery's newest vintage and helped me climb aboard.
Then, he tied Mayhem's leash to one side and Taco's to the
other and escorted all three of us inside for the night.

He walked me to my room, but ever the gentlemen, he
stayed back and fed the pups and Aslan, who gave us a good
talking to before, as expected, ignoring the fact that we existed.
I slid into my emoji pj bottoms and the largest T-shirt I could
find, slipped a headband onto my curls, and hopped down the
hall to the couch.

"Still can't walk on it?" Daniel asked as he handed me a
bowl of peanut butter popcorn that was as good as any I could
make myself.

"Nope. But maybe I'll be better by morning."

Daniel looked skeptical, but he didn't say anything. I knew,
though, that if the sprain was as bad as I thought it was, I'd be

taking a trip to the hospital for X-rays in the morning. Tonight, though, I was going to enjoy a quiet Sunday night with my guy and try to figure out what exactly was so appealing to him about watching YouTube videos of giant machinery.

I didn't get very far in that pondering, not far at all. I woke up in my own bed with Aslan on my feet and the sun on my face. The smell of bacon from the kitchen was the only thing that drew me out. My head still hurt, and I could feel, as soon as I moved my leg, that it was double its usual size. Time for X-rays.

When I hopped my way to the kitchen, Daniel was at the griddle, and I could see pancakes with the special orange sauce my mom had taught him to make and what appeared to be a whole pound of bacon. "I mean, I love the stuff, but I don't think even I can eat that many pieces of bacon."

Daniel winked at me. "Someday, I'll test that theory, but today, we're having guests."

As if on cue, my mother and father walked in, without knocking of course, and my mom beelined for me with her hands out. My mom wasn't exactly the nurturing type, but if there was a problem to solve, she was the one you wanted on your side. "Harvey Beckett, what happened to your face?"

I reached two fingers up and felt my temple and then down my cheekbone. I felt like one of those kids in an old-timey TV show who had the mumps. My face was swollen. VERY swollen. "I just fell, Mom."

She frowned. "This is not a simple fall, Harvey. I mean Daniel told us you had a hard night, but I didn't expect to find my only daughter looking like she'd been in the prize fight in Atlantic City."

"I'm fine, Mom," I said as I jumped down from the bar stool and immediately collapsed with a cry of pain.

Daniel rushed around and lifted me up, half guiding and half carrying me to the couch.

"Well, if that's fine, then I'm Diana Ross."

A vision of my slim, very white, not-at-all-musical mom singing "I Will Survive" in a slinky, sequined ball gown passed through my mind's eye, and I started to giggle. Then, I looked at my dad, and he snorted as the laughter he'd been holding in burst forth. Soon, all four of us were in the midst of one of those laughing spells that almost always leads to someone rushing to the facilitates before they have an accident.

When we all quieted, Daniel looked at me and said, "But seriously, Harvey—"

I didn't let him finish. "Please just give me the dignity of bacon and pancakes before I go to the ER, okay?"

"Deal," he said as he slipped two fluffy cakes onto a plate, doused them with orange sauce, and slid bacon beside them. At my feet, two hound dogs looked doleful, but I averted my eyes and held my plate aloft while I chowed down. Dad and Mom sat at the island behind me, and Daniel perched himself on the kitchen counter. It was a very casual but somehow just perfect Monday morning breakfast . . . well, except for the sneaking suspicion that was growing in my mind and my right leg that I may have something more than a sprain.

After breakfast, I sent Daniel off to work with our two canine charges and the promise that he'd bring them by the shop to meet and greet this afternoon, even if I didn't make it in. Mondays were busy. Then, I called Marcus, who was already scheduled to open, and let him laugh hysterically about Max's blundering idiocy before I told him I had to go to the hospital. To his credit, he did as he always did and promised to keep things moving but also to check in if he needed me.

Then, I let Dad help me to the car while Mom gave Aslan a can of tuna *in oil* and solidified their slightly controlling but ever loveable identity as soul sisters, feline and human together. As we drove, I caught my parents up on the weekend's wild escapades. They'd been away in Boston for the weekend, an anniversary getaway, and I'd resisted the urge to text them about everything because I wanted them to have fun. But as predicted, my mom was upset I hadn't let them know and Dad was pleased I hadn't. They were both more relaxed than I'd seen them in a while, though, so I decided I'd made the right choice.

Mom was already planning how she would coordinate a parallel event for the night with John Green. Mom had made her mark on Baltimore as quite the philanthropic event planner, and I was always glad when she threw her expertise in my direction. Today, her idea was to set up a booth by the bookstore and ask people about the three things they wanted people to remember about them after they died. She'd record their stories, anonymously or not as the guest preferred, and then she'd produce a podcast – something she'd wanted to do for a long time – of the recordings. "I've been really wanting to start a podcast, and this is perfect."

"Yes, dear, but how is that a fundraiser?" Dad asked as I thought the same question but was too chicken to verbalize it.

"Oh, right. Yes, well, I'll donate all the advertising proceeds to hospice, of course. It may take a while to get those funds rolling in, but hopefully, the income stream would be longstanding if not huge." She turned to stare out the window, and I knew we'd lost her to her plans.

I leaned forward from the back seat and put my hand on Dad's shoulder. "Thanks for taking me, Dad."

"Of course, honey. I just wish we didn't have to. Why can't that man just leave you alone?"

"If I knew that, Dad, I would have made it happen a long time ago." I sat back and watched the flat land of the Eastern Shore whiz by.

TWO HOURS LATER, a CT scan showed I didn't have a concussion, but an X-ray revealed a broken ankle. They'd given me some pain medication – the good stuff – and I was waiting in the ER lobby again for the doctor to come, be sure the bone was set properly, and wrap my leg in a cast up to my knee. I was secretly a little thrilled at the prospect of having my friends sign the cast and then Cate and Henri decorating around the signatures. As a kid, I'd always wanted a broken bone – or rather the attention that came with it – but until this moment, at age forty-five, I had never so much as broken a toe. It was my lucky day, especially now that I had those pain meds in my system.

Mom and Dad had gone to the cafeteria in search of lunch, and I was grateful for a break from all the fussing over me. I liked the attention, of course, but the pestering and controlling about what I was going to do now that I was in a cast, that was wearing me down. I had just picked a copy of *Better Homes and Gardens*, a magazine that I should just subscribe to but never do because I'm afraid I won't enjoy waiting room copies as much then, when I heard shouting voices from the hallway.

As I watched, a man in his thirties with olive skin and black hair came around the corner with a curly haired nurse in pink scrubs right behind him. "Mr. Petra, wait. Please," she said.

"No, I'm done with you people. You let that monster of a human being have unfettered access to my father, and now my father is dead. I am suing. Someone needs to take responsibility." The man stormed out the emergency room doors, or he would have if there was really a way to make a dramatic exit through doors that open automatically.

I kept my face down toward my magazine, but over the top of it, I watched the nurse sink into a chair. I was the only one in the waiting room – apparently Monday mornings aren't big emergency moments in our parts – and she seemed to just need to take a break. I eyed the unopened bottle of water beside me and decided it was worth the sacrifice. So I scooped it up and hopped over and sat two chairs from the nurse. "You okay?" I asked.

She looked startled, like she hadn't noticed me before. But then her face softened. "Yeah," she reached over and took the water I held out, "Just some things are really hard."

I nodded and held up my leg that was wrapped up like the mummy's lost appendage. "Tell me about it."

She cracked a wry smile then and took a sip of the water.

"I hope you don't think I'm rude, but I heard what that man said . . . and, well, I was wondering," there really wasn't a delicate way to say this, "um, was he talking about Nurse Bixley."

A crease formed between her eyebrows, and she started to stand.

"Sorry. I just know about the case because he died in my store."

The nurse lowered herself back into her seat and said, "Oh, that bookstore on Main. I need to stop in."

"Please do. But please also know that I'm not just trying to be nosy. I really just want to be sure that whoever did this is caught."

She nodded and then looked down at her hands. Her voice grew very quiet. "Javier's father, Ramone, was a regular patient here. He had cancer – I really shouldn't be telling you this, you know?"

"I do know, and I don't need any medical details of course. And really, you don't have to tell me anything if you don't want to." I was being honest, but I also really, really hoped she'd tell me."

"It will probably help me to talk about it. Everything here is so hush hush because everyone is afraid of a lawsuit." She met my eyes for the first time, and I could see she looked like she might cry.

I put my hand on her arm. "Yeah." I really didn't want to

pressure her, but I felt like whatever she had to say was probably important.

She took a deep breath and said. "Every few months, Ramone would be back in, his white count too high, his pain excruciating, and each time, we'd get him a transfusion and some good rest with pain medication. It was only a matter of time, of course, but the doctors figured he had another few months at least." The nurse shoved her hands into the pockets of her scrubs and stretched the fabric against her fists. "One night, though, when we were a bit short-handed, Ramone coded, and we couldn't bring him back."

"But since you all knew he still wasn't *that* sick, it worried you?" I didn't want to press too hard, but there was something here.

"Exactly. Javier pushed for an autopsy, said his father's death was suspicious, but his sister Esme was managing their father's affairs and decided against it." She stood then and looked like she was about to leave. "I might not think Javier was right, you know, if this wasn't the third time I personally saw this happen." She gave me a wan smile and turned to go.

"Wait, the third time what happened?"

She looked around the room then, suddenly aware of where we were, it seemed. But then she leaned over and said quietly in my ear, "The third time someone died when we were short-handed on a shift." Then, she turned and walked away.

I started to call after her, to tell her my name, to ask hers, but I stopped short. It seemed wiser to not know who she was, more deniability for her since she probably broke a bunch of rules of medical ethics there . . . and I needed to call Tuck.

7

The sheriff didn't waste any time in coming to hear what I had to say. Before the doctor finished the last wrap of plaster on my cast, my friend was sitting beside me, waiting. When the doctor left to mix the epoxy he was going to put on my leg to make it "sea-worthy," I said, "I absolutely cannot tell you what I know here. Definitely not. You'll have to wait."

"No problem," he said, taking his phone out of his pocket. "I just got a new Sudoku app, and I brought the cruiser today. So I can give you and your bum leg a ride home."

I smiled and took out my own phone. This jigsaw puzzle wasn't going to finish itself.

By the time the indigo blue epoxy was dry enough for me to risk rubbing it against a passerby and not adhering to them permanently, I was on to a new puzzle, this one an absurdly hard one of bookshelves full of books that did not have any titles. It was going to take me forever, which was just fine since I was going to be largely chair-bound for the next four to six weeks until I could get my walking cast. Looked like I was going to be on crutches for Christmas. Oh joy!

Tuck helped me get settled onto the instruments apparently designed to torture my armpits, and then he carried my messenger bag while I made my way slowly, oh so slowly, down the hallway to his waiting car. He opened the back door for me, and I thought he was joking. Then, I saw that his passenger seat was full of a laptop contraption thingy. As if it wasn't humiliating enough that I broke my ankle trying to get away from the skeezy dude who had a crush on me, now I was going to ride to my place of business in the back of a squad car. I was seriously in need of an infusion of the holiday spirit ASAP.

On the short drive, I filled Tuck in on what the nurse told me – through the perforated plexiglass – and was again grateful that I hadn't asked her name when he asked me for it. "I don't know. She didn't tell me."

Tuck squinted at me in the rearview mirror and said, "Is this one of those 'don't ask, don't tell' things?"

"Precisely," I quipped, "but without the rampant homophobia and prejudice."

When Tuck pulled up to the bookstore, there was a small greeting committee. Walter and Stephen were leading the way with, oh glory, a wheelchair, and Rocky was on hand with a mug, a steaming mug, and all I could think was, "Dear God, please let that be a peppermint mocha."

Mom helped me out of the car. The errands that she and Dad had left to do when they'd dropped me at the hospital apparently involved me and the nursing care they felt I needed. Mom steered me toward Stephen, who was ready and very eager to drive my wheelchair when, just in time, Elle Heron rolled up on a knee scooter, and I literally cheered.

I'd seen people in casts use these in the store – they look just like a child's scooter but with a knee-high cushion meant for you to rest your calf on while you used your fully functional leg to propel yourself around. I was almost excited about having a broken ankle when I saw it, and once I hopped my way over to Elle – Mom refused to give me back my crutches as if that would get me to sit in the wheelchair festooned in streamers and complete with a lap blanket – I hugged her and took off down the sidewalk with a whoop.

No one needed to know the whoop was also one of pain because, well, it hurt like crap to put any weight on my broken leg. I was still going to enjoy this baby, just maybe a little later.

I scooted my way back to Dad, who had done me the courtesy of undecorating the wheelchair, and let him wheel me into the store. Apparently, my grand return to work was not going to be limited to the massive public spectacle on the sidewalk. Nope, inside Marcus had already drawn up my favorite wingback chair and set up the cash register with a special café table counter so that I could greet customers, ring up sales, and look up special orders, all without having to stand. If it wasn't all so darn embarrassing, I might have thanked him. But instead, I tried to look grateful as Woody, Henri and Bear, Cate and Lucas, and even Daniel cheered – with actual claps and shouts – when I stood, turned, and dropped into my new throne. It might have been unbearable, but I didn't see a scepter or a tiara in sight. So really, it was just humiliating.

I had to admit, to myself at least, though that I was grateful for the chair. The ordeal of the weekend, the injuries of last night, which still included a pounding headache, combined with what I'd just learned at the hospital, had left me knackered, to use one of Mart's favorite expressions. But I put on a brave face, let my friends and parents fuss over me a bit, and then sent them on their way so that I could, "Run my store." I said it with gusto, but really, I just wanted to be with my books and my sales figures so I could rest.

Everyone took the not-so-subtle hint and started to head out, but my mother, of course, darted back to hang a makeshift bouquet of bows she'd salvaged from the wheelchair on the scooter that Elle had parked next to my throne. I felt like one of those women who save the bows from their wedding shower and use them as a makeshift bouquet at their wedding rehearsal, but without any reason to have such a bouquet . . . well beyond my mother's clear desire to force me to look silly. Still, I kissed her cheek and thanked her when she left . . . and then as soon as she was out the door, I nailed a three-pointer in the trashcan behind the actual cash register.

THE AFTERNOON WENT BY SWIMMINGLY, and I only had to endure the throbbing pain in my leg once, when bathroom require-ments necessitated I get scooting. Otherwise, I sat in my throne and recommended books to accompany the ones people brought up to purchase while Marcus staffed the floor, offering tips and reading commiseration as always.

My favorite customer of the day was buying a complete set of the original Nancy Drew series, and for a fleeting moment, I wished Mom was here to see it. She had read all Keene's books when she was a little girl, and I still had her original copies – less a few that went missing over the years – in my own library. The woman buying them looked to be about my mother's age, but I knew better than to presume, so I asked, "Buying these for yourself?"

"Oh no. I have my originals at home. These are for my grandsons. They love mysteries, and if you love mysteries, you *must* meet Nancy."

She spoke with such affection that I almost missed that she said "grandsons," but when I pointed out that many a person of her generation might presume Nancy was only for girls.

"Pish. Gender is a construct anyway. And we need men who appreciate what a woman can do, don't you think?"

"Yes, ma'am," I said, and then asked her about the new

Nancy Drew TV series and her thoughts. She, like me, thought it was good television, a strong contemporary nod to the original books, but a little too scary for our taste.

I watched her and her tweed cape as she left the store and felt better than I had all day, and not just because we had sold fifty-six books to one customer.

By the time seven o'clock came, both Marcus and I were beyond ready to close up shop. He had stayed, out of kindness, because, well, I needed him to stay. He was always going way beyond the call of duty (and the expectations of his salary), and as he turned off the neon sign and tidied the café with Rocky, I realized two things: he needed a raise, and we needed another bookseller.

I immediately thought of Tiffany, a runner friend of Mart who had mentioned when we'd had drinks last week that she was looking for some extra work to help cover holiday expenses. She was reliable, well-read, and fun. She'd be a blast to have in the store, and I knew the customers would love her. Moreover, I needed someone to be my legs while I was ensconced in my throne of bookish delight. I picked up my phone and texted, "Interested in being my new bookseller for December?"

"When do you need me? I can start tomorrow."

She and I made plans for her to come in at nine the next morning, when I could train her, and then she'd work my shifts with me for the rest of the month. If the number of emojis in her messages were any indicator, she was excited, and I was, too. I liked Tiffany, and it would be good to have help if our banner day of sales was any indication. Plus, Santa would be back this weekend, and I expected we'd have some massive lines to contend with. My only worry was overhead, but I would have to figure that out later.

The next morning, Tiffany was early, mega early, so early

that I had barely sipped my latte when she knocked robustly on the front door Someone was clearly still excited.

I unlocked the door and quickly stepped back as she barreled in with her arms full of tote bags. She dropped them in the nearest chair and spun toward me with a smile. "I'm here, boss," she said with more enthusiasm then I mustered on even my best day.

"I can see that, and I'm glad." I risked burning my tongue to get an extra jolt of caffeine before I said, "You don't have to come early, you know?"

"Oh, okay. Just wanted to make a good first impression." A flash of pink spread across the bridge of her nose.

I chuckled. "You already have the job, my friend. No worries there." I walked toward the café. "Latte? It's my morning tradition."

"Sure, if you don't mind, Rocky," Tiffany said.

"Not at all. Oat milk and stevia, right?" Rocky took pride in remembering everyone's drink choices after only one visit

"You got it!" Tiffany was pretty much beaming, and I suspected that she may have already done the unthinkable this morning: gone for a run.

Rocky looked at me and said, "Clearly, Tiffany will do the morning shifts?" She winked at Tiffany as she handed her the far-too-healthy latte with a mistletoe made in the foam.

"Clearly," I said with an exaggerated drawl. "Heck, I might have her open every morning if she's this, um, bouncy."

Tiffany laughed. "Sorry. I only ran six miles this morning, so I didn't get all the extra energy out yet."

Rocky and I groaned in unison. "*Only* six miles," I said. "I'd need to lie down for the rest of the day."

"Wait until the days I do a full twenty. I'm much less 'bouncy' then." Tiffany's voice was totally sincere.

"If by 'less bouncy' you mean hospitalized and on IV fluids, then me, too," Rocky said. "Enjoy the lattes."

Tiffany and I returned to the café, and apparently Mayhem had picked up on Tiffany's vivaciousness because my dog was waiting, her tail banging against the rack of greeting cards nearby, by Tiffany's bags. "She must smell the homemade dog treats I brought."

"You brought homemade dog treats?" I sighed. "I may have to give you *my* job."

Tiffany gave Mayhem a treat the size of my hand, and then looked at me. "Well, maybe just your dog."

I grinned when Mayhem got up and moved over to sit by me, as if she understood. "Sorry, it'll take more than one treat to win my girl."

"Good girl," she said. "Now, what's first?"

I swigged the rest of my latte and got to it. By the time I'd trained Tiffany on the register, helped her see how to special order a book for a customer, reviewed our upcoming book clubs and events, and briefed her on the John Green event, the poor woman looked exhausted. "It's a lot. You don't have to get it all now," I said.

"It is a lot. But I've got it. I might be at capacity for information, though. Mind if I straighten the shelves some?" she asked as she bounced on the balls of her feet.

"Mind? Please, be my guest. If you feel like it, you could even try your hand at a table display." I pointed to the table I'd cleared so we could display Greene's books.

"Really? Ooh, I love hands-on stuff. Are the books in the back?"

"Yep. Work your magic," I said.

To be honest, I hated figuring out the logistics of those displays. I just couldn't imagine what it might look like, so I had to put it together over and over again until it looked right. It was physically exhausting for me. But with Tiffany's physical energy, I figured she'd enjoy it.

While she carted the books to the front on our library truck,

I took a lap before flipping on the neon sign and unlocking the door. I'd probably never match Tiffany for kinesthetic perk, but nothing charged me quite like that first moment of the day when anything could happen in *my* bookstore. And anything usually did.

8

M arcus came in about eleven, and I re-introduced him to Tiffany before pointing out the truly stellar display of John Green's books. "Great work," he said. "You can see all the titles, but the display also works as a whole to draw readers in."

"Yeah, I was going for a "What's that? OOH, I love John Green, and wait he's coming *here* thing. I did have one question though. See how this—" I wandered off as Tiffany and Marcus nerded out on stack heights and tiers. I was so glad Marcus now had someone else to obsess over that stuff with.

I wandered with my empty mug back to Rocky's café and took a seat. The store was still pretty quiet – typical for a winter day early in the week – and I wanted a minute to think about Bixley's murder, or more specifically, the murders it looked like he had committed. I didn't condone the fact that someone had killed him, but I could understand why they had.

Still, I couldn't figure out why someone at the hospital hadn't launched an official investigation sooner. I meant Javier Petra seemed so sure what had happened to his dad, and the nurse wasn't balking about her accusations either. So why hadn't someone put a stop to what Bixley was doing? Surely, he could have been suspended pending an investigation. It just seemed really odd, but I didn't know enough about hospital operations to figure this out.

Fortunately, I knew someone who did, and double fortunately, I needed to see said someone today to give him the portion of the flyers we needed him and Henri to plaster all over the Eastern Shore. I stopped by to see Marcus, who was recommending *The Woman Upstairs* by Claire Messud to a young woman in the longest scarf I had ever seen. "People really laid into the author because she wrote a protagonist who wasn't super likeable – if by likeable you mean perky and cheerful – but I loved this book. I felt like it caught something about isolation and friendship and identity that we all know but can't always put into words."

I often thought Marcus could be a professional book reviewer, and more than once, I'd suggested he reach out to Michael Dirda, my favorite book critic, to ask about a mentorship. But he kept saying he just wanted to sell books, not write about them. More and more, though, I thought he could really do something with book reviews. So I'd talked with his mom, who was our resident book reviewer in our store newsletter, and she'd convinced Marcus to take on one or two reviews a month starting in January. I couldn't wait to see what he said, and I knew our readers would gobble up his insightful, wise commentary. We'd sell books from his reviews, I knew, but more, I was just excited to see him use his considerable talent for understanding a book's larger implications for a wider audience.

The woman, of course, bought the Messud novel, which Tiffany rang up carefully, and then I grabbed Marcus. "You okay holding down the fort? I need to step out for a couple of hours."

"Of course. I will, however, need more caffeine. That Tiffany—"

"I know," I said. "You should see her at eight forty-five."

"I don't want to," Marcus said as he headed toward the café, where Rocky was already pulling a double espresso as if she could read her boyfriend's mind.

I grabbed my bag from the back, leashed up Mayhem, and headed out with my scooter under my leg. I decided to stop by Daniel's place. He and Taco were napping on the tufted leather sofa at the back of his garage, and when Mayhem jumped up beside them and laid down, I laughed. "Mind if she stays?" I asked when Daniel pried open one eye.

"Nope. I'll bring her by later. We'll just be here, resting our eyes," he said before letting out a long sigh and closing his eye again.

I really wanted to curl up with them, but I knew Bear would probably only be at the hospital for a bit longer. He usually worked mornings and then spent his afternoons at the free clinic up in Easton. Henri had once told me, "He makes a pittance there, but it fills his soul. That's what counts." I really wanted to see him in action at the clinic, but I didn't have the time for the drive today. I picked up the pace and took advantage of my toughening leg muscles to let the scooter carry me down the sidewalk.

I got a couple of cheers from people I whizzed by, and I wondered if this is what skateboarders felt like when they zoomed down the sidewalk. I'd have to remember to ask Marcus, who was pretty good on a board. In no time, I was paddling my way into the ER like I was the coolest girl in town, and by the time I pulled up to the counter and asked for Bear, I felt downright cool, which was not a feeling I often had or even thought about. But now that I had it, it was, well, cool.

The nurse at the desk said, "Take a seat, Speedy" and gave me a wink as I slid back into my all-too-familiar waiting room chair and picked up *Southern Living*. There was an article on cottage gardens that could inspire me to attempt something I could barely keep up with come spring.

I was able to read that whole article plus one on the best frozen green pepper recipes before Bear had a moment to step away and speak to me. I pulled the flyers out of my satchel and handed them to him, and then I asked if I could take him to lunch. He glanced at his watch and then caught the eye of the nurse at the desk. She gave me a smile and a nod. "I know where to find you," she said.

"Guess I'm all yours?" he said with a smile. "But I'm afraid I can't leave the grounds. So cafeteria food, okay?"

"More than okay. That chicken Caesar wrap they constructed for me the other day was phenomenal. This is not the hospital food I've heard rumors of."

Bear grinned. "We save that food for the actual patients who have no choice. If you can walk away, we want to coax you to spend even more of your money here, so we make good food." There was just the tiniest hint of bitterness in Bear's voice, and I made a mental note to explore that at another date.

After I got another wrap – when I find something I like, I consume it until I can't stand the sight of it – and Bear helped himself to a piece of barbecue chicken pizza and a bottle of water, he got right to business. "So you finally here to figure out the scoop with Bixley?"

I shrugged and tried to look casual, but Bear wasn't buying it. "Don't bat those eyelashes at me, Missy. I'm onto you."

I laughed and shrugged. "I can't deny it, Bear. Something seems off with all this. If so many people were dying, why wasn't the hospital doing anything about it?"

He lowered his voice and sat forward a bit. "Same reason we have this nice cafeteria that's open to the public."

"Money?" I whispered. The knot in my throat made it hard for me to swallow my chicken. "What do you mean?"

He leaned forward even more and said, "Two things. First, the longer people are in the hospital, the more the hospital can charge the insurance."

"So the hospital makes more money."

He nodded. "Secondly, word of an angel of mercy gets out . . ."

"And donors go away, investigations are launched, people sue."

He put his finger to his nose. "That last one especially." He rolled his pizza up and took a big bite, chewing carefully and swallowing before saying, "This is all bad news, very bad news for everyone, but the hospital rationalizes their lack of inquiry as being about the greater good."

I frowned. "You mean they say things like, 'Sacrificing the few for the many.'"

Bear sighed. "It doesn't have to be one or the other, though. We could have caught Bixley and still cared for most people, even if we had to settle a lawsuit or two with his first victims. Instead, we let him keep killing with the hopes we wouldn't have to do anything."

"Who is the 'we' here, Bear?"

Bear sat back and looked around. "I know this is going to sound paranoid, Harvey," he whispered. "But everyone."

"Everyone?" My voice got suddenly louder than I expected, and Bear winced. "What do you mean?"

"I mean there isn't a person at this hospital, including me, who hadn't heard something about what Bixley was doing. All of us could have asked for an inquiry, and if enough of us had, we would have gotten one. But most of us stayed quiet, and so here we are. At least ten patients dead and him, too."

I slowly ate the rest of my wrap as I thought about what Bear said. The entire hospital knew that Bixley was murdering people, and no one did anything. I was appalled, but then something Bear said snagged in my mind. "You say 'most' of you stayed quiet. Did anyone speak up?"

One corner of Bear's mouth twisted up. "Caught that did you? Good girl. Yes, someone filed an anonymous complaint to the ethics board. They are obligated to investigate, so they did a cursory job. They didn't uncover anything conclusive about Bixley's actions, so the case was dropped."

"How do you know this, Bear?" I wasn't sure I wanted the answer, but it also felt important.

"I am on the ethics board." His face was solemn, and his eyes pleading. "So you see . . ."

"And I thought it was personal before. I'm so sorry, Bear." I studied my friend across the table and thought about how kind he was, how generous, how very moral. I knew this must be tearing him up. "You've told all this to Tuck?"

"First thing, Harvey." He leaned across the table and put his large hand over mine. "If I hadn't, I wouldn't be telling you, Sleuth Girl. Tuck is already looking into it, so you don't have to. You may be cool as ice on that scooter, but we do not need you getting in the way of a killer."

I felt a shiver run up my spine. "I hear you, Bear. And I'm not trying to investigate per se. But this thing about multiple murders happening in a hospital, it was bugging me. Made me nervous to tell you the truth. I come here for care, after all."

Bear's face grew soft and even more sorrowful. "I know. That's the really sad part. People will now be afraid to come here because if this can happen once . . ."

This time I put my hand over Bear's. "Tuck will catch the killer, and then, perhaps there can be justice for all the victims, even Bixley."

"I hope so, Harvey. I hope so." Bear stood and bussed our table as I got myself steady again on my scooter. My antics from earlier had made my broken ankle throb, and there were ligaments in my hips that were very unhappy with me. Still, I managed to make my way back to the ER with Bear without wincing too much.

As I was about to scoot out the automatic doors, I hugged my friend and caught a glimpse of my regular chair here in the waiting room. I realized I'd never told Bear about what the nurse had shared about Javier Petra. I gave him the full story, and he nodded most of the way. "Yes, Javier has a real temper. No doubt. And he had good reason to be angry. Still, I don't know that he could so this." Bear squinted at me. "My turn to ask – you told Tuck?"

"Right away," I said. "He's looking into it."

"Good." He bent down and hugged me again. "Now, I'm headed to put a flyer in every break room in this hospital. We need a full house for Mr. Green."

I smiled and waved as I scooted back to the shop, wincing all the way.

9

When I arrived, Daniel, Mayhem, and Taco were just approaching, too, and they waited for me as I slowly scooted the last few yards. I must have looked pained because Daniel slipped an arm around me and shifted my weight off the scooter and onto him, even as he deftly maneuvered two hound dogs to his other hand. "You okay?" he asked. "You're very pale."

"I may have overdone it," I said with another wince. "Take me to my throne." I tried to sound regal, but my voice was hoarse with agony. "And bring me my royal pills."

Daniel rolled his eyes and half-carried me to my wingback chair before going to the break room to find the bottle of ibuprofen I'd told him was in my purse. When he returned, he bowed and said, "My Lady" as he handed me two red pills and then trotted off in search of water and coffee at my behest.

When he returned, I caught him up on what Bear had said. "So there's some sort of profit motive involved, huh? Surprise, surprise." Daniel was, at heart, an optimist, but when it came to all things business, he was a cynic through and through. While he ran his garage ethically and with a generous heart toward his customers, he had come to understand that many people in the world were just out to grab all they could. It was the one shard of bitterness he carried, and I was afraid this time he was right.

"That's what Bear thinks anyway. He's pretty sure that there's a sort of passive cover-up of Bixley's actions—"

"Hey, you two," Damien interrupted so suddenly that I jumped a few inches off my seat. "Oh sorry. I thought you saw me coming."

I looked around quickly and wondered how in the world he had thought that given that he had come up behind me.

Daniel shot me a quizzical stare and then stood to shake hands with our in-house Santa. "How you are doing?"

"Just fine. Great, actually." He turned to me. "That's why I'm here. I wanted to ask if you'd thought about having Santa for a couple more nights a week. Seems I've made quite the impression." He held up his phone and scrolled up through his Instagram feed. It was full of him in his Santa hat taking selfies with people on the street. "It's incredible, right?"

"Incredible is one word for it," I said. "People are stopping you on the street to have their picture with you because a man died in your lap." I felt like my voice was full of disgust, but either I was more subtle than I thought or Damien wouldn't know disgust if it hit him in the face.

"Yep. I'm kind of a celebrity. I mean, not like that Pattinson guy or anything, but still."

For a minute, I got the image of Robert Pattison as a glittery vampire Santa and almost started to laugh, but my discomfort with Damien's ability to revel in this reason to be the center of attention overrode the giggles. "So you want me to pay you to work extra nights because you want to satisfy your adoring fans?" Again, there was a definite sneer to my words, but also again, Damien seemed oblivious.

"Yep, could we? I mean I think you'd probably make a lot

more money than you pay me, especially if I plug your books. Maybe you could set up a display of true crime books around me or something?"

I was halfway out of my chair and ready to drop my cast on Damien's toe when Daniel stepped in. "I'm not sure that books about serial killers and notorious murderers are exactly the right thing for the Christmas mood Harvey is going for here, Damien."

For a split second, Damien frowned, and I was hopeful that maybe mild fame hadn't obliterated all of his good judgment. But nope, clearly, he was stupefied by his own glamorousness because he said, "Well, maybe I could just recommend them to people. You know, help you boost your sales?"

I rolled my eyes. "Let me think about it, okay?" I am a total pushover most of the time, far too quick to make people happy, so I'd learn to say, "Let me think about it" when I even had a slight hesitation about something and really wanted to be sure that I did, in fact, want to do what I was already leaning toward doing anyway. "I'll text you later."

"Cool," Damien said and then walked to the door, where he stopped and peered out as if he was going to have to make a break for it past the paparazzi.

"Unbelievable," I said.

Daniel grinned. "It's like we have our own reality show, *The Eastern Shore*, but instead of 'The Situation' we have 'Murder Santa.'" He winked at me.

I groaned. "I have never seen that show and will never, but if teen girls start showing up here for autographs with Damien, Santa will have to retire for the year."

"So noted," Marcus said as he walked up. "Have you seen his Insta?"

I rolled my eyes again and was glad I'd long ago disproved the childhood rumor that my eyes would stick that way if I did it too much.

"You follow him on Instagram?" Daniel said.

"Yep. You don't? He plugs the store all the time. Two people came in this afternoon, in fact, just to see when he'd next be here."

"Were they wearing all black or carrying ski masks?" I asked with weariness.

Marcus laughed. "Actually, they were reporters eager to do a story about what a business owner does when something terrible happens during the happiest time of the year." Marcus wiggled his eyebrows at me.

"Really?! Now, that's a reasonable angle on this story." I looked over at Daniel. "What do you think? Maybe I can, as they say, control the narrative a little."

"Seems reasonable to me," my boyfriend said as he gave me a kiss on the cheek and stood. "I'll see you in the papers."

"I think the expression is, "I'll see you in the funny papers,'" Marcus said.

"Oh, I know." Daniel smiled, patted Taco on the head, and headed out the door.

"Glad you think it's a good idea, because the reporters and their camera crew will be here in . . . ," he looked at the clock hanging on the back wall of the store, "fifteen minutes."

"Marcus! Seriously. Look at me?!" My hair was pulled back with a loose piece of ribbon left over from a package I'd wrapped for a customer the night before. I had one heck of a shiner still, and then there was the cast. "I cannot go on camera like this."

"Don't worry. I called in help." Marcus swaggered away to help an older man who was exploring our books on cats just as Tiffany and Cate swooped in with bags.

"I've got the hair," Tiffany said.

"I'm on make-up," Cate added.

Before I could even say "Hi," they were on me, and I felt like I was in a make-up trailer. For a split second, I thought, *Don't let*

Damien see this. He'll want his own team, and then the giggles that always sat right behind my tears when I'm under stress broke loose and my two stylists had to fight my bouncing shoulders while they worked.

Still, by the time they were done and had pulled out not one but two mirrors, I looked not only presentable but downright professional. Cate had perfectly masked the growing bruise on my face, and Tiffany had somehow managed my curls into a wave that covered the worst of the still-present goose egg while pinning back the other side. I looked good, especially with the blue stripe of hair that I had really grown to love showing just enough to make me look cool but not reckless.

"Wow! Thanks, women." I started to stand up to hug them, but the weight of my cast kept me from rising all the way. "Oh no, my cast. I know very little about being on camera, but I don't really want people seeing this bright blue thing in every shot."

Just then, I saw two women in blue suits walk in with a cameraman and a woman with one of those long, stick-like microphones – a boom, it was called maybe – in hand. I groaned.

"Don't worry, Harvey. I've got this," Cate said as she stood, quickly wiped her hands on her apron, and walked over to greet the reporters.

I watched with growing anxiety as the women talked, and Tiffany stood behind me to rub my shoulders. "They're just here to see the woman who can still run a store after a murder and a broken ankle. You're already impressive just by being here, Harvey. Just be yourself."

I smiled up at my friend and felt, for about the millionth time, such gratitude for my friends. "You're right. I am impressive."

Tiffany guffawed, and I joined in. Her laugh was so infectious that it lifted my spirits immediately. I was still smiling when the reporters walked over.

"Harvey Beckett?" One of the women stuck out her hand.

I started to stand, and the other woman said. "Please not on our account. Woman, if I'd had someone die in my store and then broken my ankle all in the course of a couple of days, I'd be home with *The Umbrella Academy*, a margarita, and raw cookie dough."

I smiled. "The thought is tempting, but tell me, how is *The Umbrella Academy*? Good weird or just plain weird?"

We launched into a quick analysis of the new fantasy TV show, and I immediately began to feel at ease. If you like strange, magical powers in ensemble casts, we can be friends.

"Cate tells me you're worried about your cast on camera."

I looked at Cate, and she nodded. "Yeah, a little. Can I drape something over it or something?"

"We have a better idea. Ollie is going to sit at your feet and paint it." I looked up to see my old friend, a very talented painter and mixed media artist grinning down at me. "You game?"

"That's what we were going to do anyway, right?" Cate said.

I nodded and then felt my eyes tear. "Ollie, you're going to paint my cast? I'm honored, but you know this means I can never take it off, right?"

He laughed. "What if I paint in a zipper, so that when the doctors cut it off, it looks intentional?"

"Ooh, yes," Tiffany shouted and bounced.

"Great," one of the reporters said. "We can do this right here, right now if you're ready."

Ollie set up his paints and palette as well as a few pieces of fabric, and I got goosebumps. His mixed media stuff was amazing, and I was going to be wearing it.

"Sounds good. Can you give me a heads up about what we're going to talk about?"

The second reporter smiled. "Sure. We just want to hear about what it's like to have a tragedy hit your business during the holidays. Did you think about closing the store for a few days? What made you decide against that? That kind of thing."

I pursed my lips and said, "Got it. Okay, I'm ready."

Reporter number one smiled at me and then gave the cameraman a nod as the mic operator lowered her sound-gathering puff toward my face. "Harvey Beckett, how are you?"

I tried not to make my face look like those terrible photos that pass around Facebook all the time while I said, "I'm okay, thank you," and wished I knew the reporter's name so I would appear more friendly.

"I'm so glad to hear it," she continued, "especially after the hard few days you've had."

I saw the camera shift slightly down to capture my leg and Ollie's work, as he started in on what looked like it would be a Christmas tree. "Well," I said, looking back at the reporter and willing myself not to look into the camera directly, "the show must go on, as they say." I could not believe I had trotted out that cliché, but I kept myself from rolling my eyes at my own lack of imagination.

"Indeed," reporter two added, as she pulled up a chair just a bit in front of me and to the side. I turned toward her and hoped Tiffany's hair magic was still covering my goose egg since it was now facing the camera. "You had a really hard evening on Friday. Can you tell us about that?"

I took a long deep breath. "Sadly, a man died in my bookstore on Friday. It was a terrible tragedy." I knew I was over-selling a bit, but I didn't want to look callous.

"The man died, as we understand it," reporter one said with a glance at her partner," in Santa's lap."

I felt a wave of foreboding cross over my body, but I dismissed it. These were the facts. Probably better to just get them out there. "Yes, that's right. He did."

"Well, that must have been, well, scary, angering, frustrating?" Reporter one said, and I was suddenly glad I didn't know her name because I would have spat it at her. This was an ambush, and I knew how to evade an ambush – I stepped around it.

"Actually, it was simply profoundly sad. Any person losing their life is a tragedy. The fact that it happened in my store, well, that was just a situation. The loss of life – that's the horrible thing here."

Reporter two glanced at reporter one, and I saw them dig in to this attack. I felt Ollie look up at me, and when I looked down, he was nodding slowly. Then, I felt Tiffany's hand on my shoulder as she stepped into the frame behind me, and Cate placed herself gently on the arm of my chair. My team was ready.

"Still, though, you must have felt, well something. I mean it was the first night you had Santa in your store, and there he was with a dead body in his lap."

Tiffany squeezed my shoulder, and I said, "I did feel something. Sadness. As I said, a man died, and that is always sad."

Reporter two charged in, "But weren't you worried about your store, what this would do to your shop's reputation?"

I resisted the temptation to laugh out loud because my shop had already had its fair share of scandal. If that worried me, I'd have shut down my first week open. "No, I wasn't. I was worried that the man who collapsed in my store was getting proper medical attention. Then, I was worried about the man, I mean about Santa, who had just witnessed a man die. Finally, I was worried about the young patrons who witnessed this tragedy. But my store, that was the least of my worries." I took another long, slow breath, and then I glared at each woman in turn as I said, "I do find it interesting, however, that YOU don't seem the least bit interested in the victim or discovering who killed him."

Both women flushed beet red, and I knew I'd hit them in

the gut. Reporter one tried to stammer out something, but Cate spoke first. "Ollie seems to have captured Harvey's heart about this tragic instance very well." She caught the reporter's eye, and he panned down to show the beautiful face of Santa with a tear streaming down his cheek.

I wanted to cry myself because the painting was, of course, perfect and not only spoke to the real sentiment I had about Bixley's death but also to the people he allegedly murdered. I wasn't about to bring that up though, so I steadied my breath and looked right at the camera. "Friends and family of Mr. Bixley, I am truly sorry for your loss. The doors of All Booked Up are open to you anytime should it help you to be in this place. Know you have the deepest condolences from everyone here." As I finished, I saw a smile on the cameraman's face, and the boom operator let out a little "yes" under her breath before the reporters glared at them. Clearly, the support team wasn't totally behind the faces that got to be on camera.

I sat patiently, camera rolling, as the reporters looked at each other for a long moment before reporter one said, "Thank you so much for your time, Harvey." She looked over her shoulder and said, "Cut."

Then, I stood up with Cate at one elbow and Tiffany at the other and leaned forward as far as I could balance on one leg. "Listen, here. Do not ever come in here again. You will not use someone's death or my store and employees to drum up a sensational news story. You are despicable."

The two women shrugged and walked out, and I sagged back into the chair as the cameraman and the boom operator gave me quick high fives as they followed their bosses out the door. Tuck passed the two reporters in the doorway and nodded. Then, he headed straight for me. "What was that about?"

"That was about Harvey schooling some nosy reporters about what really matters," Marcus said with sheer pride. "And

I got it all on tape. Already loaded it to my Insta and sent it to Galen, too. Sorry, though, I didn't know they were going to go after you like that."

"How could you? I'm fine, but you may not be. Did you just say you uploaded that to video?" If I hadn't been so tired I would have tried to leap from my chair again, but the weight of the past few days held me down. "You did not?"

"Oh yes, he did, and I shared it," Rocky piped in from over at the café. "I'm up to thirty likes already."

"Yep, you're going viral, Ms. Beckett." Mart was standing in the doorway of the shop with a grin on her face, "and I am here for it."

This time I did pry myself to standing so I could hug Mart. "What are you doing here? I thought you weren't coming back until tomorrow."

"I heard about your fall, and I told my client I needed to get home to care for my roommate. They totally understood and sent a 'get well' bottle." She held up a shimmering bottle of rosé and smiled.

For about the fiftieth time that day, I felt tears prick my eyes. "Thank you." I sat back down and looked at the friends gathered around me. "Thank you all." I propped my leg on the stool Cate had brought over and looked at the painting that Ollie had done. "This is amazing, Ollie. I don't ever want to take it off."

The young man smiled. "Trust me. You'll be ready when the itching starts. But don't worry – just like I said, I put on a zipper, so you can peel it away and keep the art."

I laughed when I twisted my leg enough to glimpse the back. Sure enough, Santa had a big ole zipper going up the back of his red suit. I loved it.

"Now, folks, if you've got things here under control, I need to get our girl home to a movie night with this fine bottle," Mart said, and Cate and Tiffany helped me to my feet. "You two – see you at six?"

"Wouldn't miss it," Cate said. "Henri and Elle are coming too. Rocky, you'll be there, right?"

"Yep, as soon as I close up. I'm not missing a Hallmark movie marathon that involves wine," she said.

I laughed. "So we're really doing this?"

"Of course we are," Mart said. "Now, let's get you home."

Tuck held open the door. "Lu's got your dinner covered. You women have fun." He leaned over to me as I passed. "Good work with those reporters, Harvey. I just watched the video. Well done." His voice was soft but sincere, and I smiled as I scooted my way to Mart's car.

10

Fifteen minutes later I was home on my couch in my softest pajama pants and largest T-shirt as Mart heated up butternut squash soup, made croutons with butter and garlic, and ordered me to sit still with a glass of wine. Aslan had no trouble with this order and promptly helped me comply by sitting on my lap. Mayhem, slightly put out by our stubborn refusal to understand her need for elevated soft furnishing, settled for her orthopedic dog bed by the fireplace and immediately began to snore. For his part, Taco – the only male allowed tonight apparently – had decided that flat on his side by the kitchen island was a better place, lest a crumb or two fall to the floor.

I busied myself by scrolling through Instagram and then taking a little bit of pride in the video Marcus shot of my interview. For the sake of trying to seem humble, I paid attention to the faces of the two shrews who had set me up, and their expressions were worth reliving the experience. If they'd been one of those montage memes, the expressions would have been a continuum from arrogant to tentative to befuddled to downright shocked to all-out mad. I reveled a bit and then flipped over to Galen's page, where the story that included the video was up to four hundred comments, all of them supportive except for the one person who felt I should have been more respectful and not commented at all. There was always someone.

I sent Galen a quick private message to thank him, and he replied immediately to say that while he knew that I meant what I said, I couldn't have possibly manufactured a better way to get publicity. He was actually going to be hosting a casual meet-up with some of his fans at the store tomorrow at noon, and he wanted to know if I could join them. "People want to meet you and give you their thanks for honoring human life like you did."

I smiled and told him that of course I'd love to meet them and that I'd love to offer his followers a ten percent discount on any purchase as my thanks for their support. Within five seconds, the discount was announced, and the likes were rolling in. I could have watched the hearts stack up all night, but I knew that what I needed to do was wind down, not get keyed up. So I tucked my phone so deep into the cushions of the couch that I couldn't even feel it vibrate and began to peruse the Hallmark movie options. My principle question was: mystery or straight-up romance?

I decided I was in the mood for mystery, and so when my friends began arriving, I asked them each to take one of the notecards that Mart had laid out on the counter. "You need to write down the clues you find, and when you think you know who the killer is, put the card in the middle of the coffee table. We'll leave the cards in order and then find out who figured it out first at the end of the movie."

Henri laughed as she picked up her card. "Where do you come up with this stuff, Harvey? I feel like we're playing a game of Clue."

"Oh, that's on the table for February. You can be Professor Plum."

"I do look good in purple," she said as she joined me on the couch with her glass of wine. "So I heard you put the smack down on two busybodies today."

I laughed and spent the next few minutes retelling the events to the gathering group of women. "Normally, I fold under that kind of pressure, but Tiffany and Cate bolstered my courage, and Ollie's art – well, it was just the inspiration I needed."

"Why do you think they wanted to set you up, Harvey?" Elle asked as she handed out bowls of soup with golden croutons floating on top. "I mean, the murder happened a few days ago, and given the twenty-four–hour news cycle, it's already old news. So why now?"

I took a spoonful of the delicious soup and thought about the question. I didn't have an answer. "I don't know actually."

"It's a good question," Cate said. "I mean why stir that up. They were really out to get you, but why? They didn't really have anything to gain since the story had faded from the headlines."

"Unless it hasn't really," Henri said. "Today there was a big meeting at the hospital. Apparently, the board is concerned about the PR surrounding Bixley's murder."

"You mean, they're worried they're going to look bad if it comes out that they were negligent," Mart snarked.

"Precisely," Henri said. "All the staff was put on strict orders not to talk about Bixley or anything related to his work at the hospital."

I sighed. "Just when the truth might out, someone greedy has to silence her again."

The room grew quiet as all of us ate and pondered the news about the hospital. I got the sense we were all strategizing our own ways of thwarting this rule, and I was all for that . . . but I suddenly remembered Damien's request to come be Santa for more nights and found that I couldn't decide. So I put it to the group.

"Sorry to interrupt everyone's scheming," I said with a smile that grew as I heard my friends' knowing chuckles, "but maybe you can help me make a decision about something." I told them about Damien's Instagram following, about how he was becoming a *very* minor celebrity, and even about Daniel's jokes that St. Marin's could be the site of the newest reality show with people who become famous for no reason. Then I said, "So what do you think? More Santa or just weekend Santa?"

Elle, always the business woman, said, "Well, do you think it will bring you more customers?"

"I think that's a given. From a business perspective, it makes sense. It's more the morality of it that worries me," I answered. "I don't want to do what the reporters today were accusing me of doing."

Mart leaned back against my legs. "Anyone who knows you, Harvey, knows you aren't going to use this tragedy to make a quick buck. I mean look at what you, Bear, and Henri are doing with the John Green event and hospice?"

"Right, Harvey," Cate added. "You are donating one hundred percent of your profits from book sales to hospice. No one can say you are out to take advantage of someone's death. So what is the wise thing to do here?"

I sighed. "Let Damien bring his groupies, I guess. But I'm drawing the line at elves in low-cut tops or short shorts."

Tiffany pouted. "Oh, darn, I was hoping just that outfit was a perk of my new job."

I lobbed a pillow at her and then dug my phone out of the cushions of the couch to text Damien. But I got distracted by the half-dozen messages a few dozen calls – mostly from Daniel and Tuck that I'd missed. I held up my phone so everyone could see my notifications, and, quickly, all my friends took out their silenced devices, too.

Mart was quickest on the draw. "Holy crap," she said as she stood. "There's been another murder. This time, at the hospital itself."

"Tuck is already there. He's asked all of us to stay here," Lu said.

"Is he worried it isn't safe?" Elle asked.

"He doesn't say, but if he asked, it's important," Lu said as she put the phone to her ear.

Just then, my phone vibrated in my hand. Mom. "Hi, Mom. You okay?"

"I am. Are you? I just heard the news while I was watching TV. Another murder, Harvey. Are you at home?"

"Yep, and everyone is here. Dad's still in Baltimore, right? Come over. Now." I tried to sound authoritative, but apparently, my attempt at bossiness hadn't been necessary because I heard my mother's keys immediately.

"I'll be there in ten minutes. But be aware, I'm in my pjs."

"You'll be in good company," I said and hung up to dial Daniel.

WHEN MOM ARRIVED a few minutes later, we still knew almost nothing. Apparently, a body had been found in a nurses' station, but beyond that we knew nothing about the victim or cause of death. I was puzzled about why Tuck had asked us to stay put, but like Lu said, if Tuck asked, it was because it was important.

Mart put on the kettle for tea, which was just as well since the wine was long gone and we probably all needed to be pretty sober. Mom made herself at home and dug out a bag of double-stuffed Golden Oreos from the cabinet over the fridge, and we all settled in for a bit of TV distraction. *The Umbrella Academy* was just intense enough and complicated enough to require focus but not intense in any way that related to the hard things around us, so it was perfect. Plus, who doesn't need an 80's dance song montage even on the hardest of nights?

We had just finished episode two when a knock at the door made most of us jump. I started to stand when Mart put a firm hand on my shoulder and said, "Seriously?!" as she walked – scooterless – and looked through the peephole. "It's Tuck and Daniel."

She opened the door, and the men walked in, looking weary. Mom immediately returned to the kitchen and turned on the kettle again, as I made room for Daniel, and Lu motioned for Tuck to take her seat in my reading chair. "What's going on?" Cate asked. "Why put us on lockdown?"

Lu squeezed Tuck's arm just as I saw the muscle in his jaw flex. Tuck would tell us what we needed to know as we needed to know it, and Cate's question was irking him. But I would have asked if she hadn't.

"A nurse was murdered at the hospital tonight. We don't know the exact circumstances, but it looks like the same MO as Bixley's murder." Tuck said.

"Oh, that's awful," Henri said softly. Then, she met Tuck's eyes. "I know this is selfish, but Bear had picked up someone's shift—"

"I saw him, and he's just fine. Told me to tell you he's okay and will see you in the morning." Tuck looked clear and firm as he spoke, and I saw Henri's face relax just a little.

"That is awful, Tuck," I said, "but still, I don't understand what this has to do with all of us?"

Daniel put his arm around my waist and pulled me close. "Harvey, it was the nurse who told you about Bixley."

I felt my stomach drop into my cast. "The woman who gave me information was murdered?"

T he next morning, Daniel drove me to work – partially because it was below freezing and scooting through icy streets didn't sound wise and partially because Tuck had asked him to. Apparently, the sheriff was a bit nervous that I might be the killer's next target since, apparently, I might know too much. My argument that he, too, "knew too much," if that was the case, fell on deaf ears, though, and I was not to be alone.

I wasn't thrilled about being a potential target, but I appreciated the company, especially that of a handsome mechanic who had great taste in women. "Thanks for the lift, Handsome," I said as Daniel pulled up to the curb in front of the store. "I'll see you at lunch?"

"You are impossible, Harvey Beckett. Did you think I would drive you here only to let two dogs drag you and your scooter across the sidewalk?"

I sighed. I really wasn't very good at accepting help, but he was right. So I let him carry my tote bag and walk the dogs to the door as I carefully scooted across the cement and into the store. It was like coming home to walk in that door, especially today. The warmth hit me full-force, and behind it, I smelled cinnamon and some other spice, maybe cloves. "What is that smell, Rocky?"

"Oh, it worked then?"

"What worked?" Daniel asked as he came in after letting two hounds do a little preemptory business in the parking lot next door.

"My decision to make mulled cider to sell for the rest of December. I thought it would be a fun addition to my menu, and I was hoping the smell would be homey, too." She beamed and handed me a mug full of the best-smelling drink in the world.

I blew on the liquid and watched steam spiral into the air before taking a small sip. It was heavenly. "Perfect, Rocky, and what a good business decision."

"Well," she said, "If you were upping your Santa game, the café needed to raise her standards, too, right?"

"Damien already told you?" Before collapsing into bed after the excitement of the nurse's murder the previous night, I'd shot off a quick text to Damien saying he could come in Wednesday through Sunday to be Santa if he wanted. But given that I'd sent the text about eleven thirty last night, I was surprised that even in St. Marin's the news had spread that fast.

"Oh, I don't talk to Damien," she made a sort of wince, "but it's all over his Insta."

She showed me his profile, and it had about ten posts all about his expanded hours as Santa at All Booked Up. It was my turn to wince. This wasn't exactly the way I wanted to make this announcement. I pictured a child-friendly poster, a tasteful FB post, a little sleigh with "Santa is staying in St. Marin's for some extra time with the children" Insta photo. But here was Damien, shirtless in one photo taken in a bathroom, with a hand-written sign that said, "See you Wednesday at All Booked Up."

I handed the phone back to Rocky. "Time to do a bit of damage control, I guess."

She showed the pictures to Daniel and said, "Oh, don't worry. Marcus and Galen are on it." She flipped through her phone and showed it to me again. "See?"

Sure enough, there was a cute picture of an elf in a sleigh with a little sign that said the new hours to visit Santa, and Galen had added it to his story. So it was getting lots of likes. Marcus had done something similar for Facebook, and as I turned to go to my throne by the register, I saw him coming out of the back room with a stack of fliers. He held one up, and it featured the same elf in a sleigh with her hand over her eyes as if looking into the distance. The text said, "Santa is coming. Keep an eye out." And then gave the hours of his time here. It was perfect.

"When Tiffany comes in, I thought I'd ask her to run these to the shops in town," Marcus said.

"Great idea. It'll get the word out, let Tiffany burn off some of that energy, and give me a chance to add a little caffeine to bolster this mulled cider in my belly."

Daniel leaned down and kissed my forehead. "I'll see you at noon." Then he turned to Marcus, "You remember our orders?"

Marcus nodded. "She won't be alone, Daniel. Not even for a minute."

I sighed and opened my laptop to look at yesterday's numbers. Everyone was overreacting, I was sure of it, but Tuck's orders.

I WAS JUST ABOUT AS BORED as bored can be in my throne when the front door slammed open and Javier Petra stormed toward me. I pressed myself against the back of my chair and held the leather-bound edition of *One Hundred Years of Solitude* that I'd special ordered for a customer to my chest as a shield. "Can I help you?" I asked.

"I saw you," Petra shouted as he loomed up and over me. "I saw you talking to Danita, and now she's dead."

I stared at the shouting man and was grateful to see Marcus come up behind him and slip his shoulder between me and Petra. "Sir, what can I do for you?"

"Her. That woman. She got Danita killed." Petra's voice boomed through the store, and from the corner of my eye, I saw Rocky pick up her phone. *Good woman*, I thought.

"Sir, I don't know what you are talking about. Who is Danita?" Petra didn't look like he was leaving, so I figured it was probably best to keep him talking, try to de-escalate things a bit.

"You know who she is. I saw the two of you talking in the ER the other day. Don't play dumb." He was scowling at me from over Marcus's shoulder.

Then it clicked. "Danita – was that the nurse's name? I never knew her name. Thank you," I said and meant it. I'd been feeling ashamed that I'd wanted to protect my own butt by not knowing her name, and it felt good to be able to call her something in my mind. Tuck hadn't wanted to tell me, at least not until they informed the next of kin. "Danita," I said again. "That's pretty."

Petra's face softened just a little, and I saw him let out a long slow breath. "You didn't know her name?"

"No, sir." I shrugged. "Bixley died here in my store." I imagined he knew this, but it felt like it might be helpful context just in case. "So when I heard you upset about him, I got nosy and asked questions. The nurse, Danita, was hesitant to tell me anything, but I pressed."

"You'd heard the rumors?" Petra said.

"I had. And well . . ." I sighed. "I'm sorry. It was none of my business."

Tuck barreled through the door at just that moment, and I met his gaze and gave him a slow nod to let him know we were okay. Then, I said, to be sure, "We're okay, Tuck. Mr. Petra and I – can I call you Mr. Petra? – are just talking."

"Javier. Please call me Javier." He let out a long slow breath from his nose, and I saw more of the tension slide from his shoulders. "I'm sorry. I overreacted. I thought, well, I don't know what I thought. But when I heard about Danita, I remembered you, and I'd seen that video of you and the reporters . . ."

"And you kind of lost it," Marcus said as he took a step back and out from between Javier and me.

"Right. I just kind of lost it." He met my eyes again then, but this time there was only sadness there. "I'm so sorry."

I nodded. "It's okay. I'd be angry if I were you, too. Heck, I'm angry, and no one I know died."

Tuck stepped up. "Mr. Petra? Sheriff Mason. If you have a minute, I'd like to talk to you. I was intending to do so sooner, but the case, well, it keeps getting more complicated. Now, though, I think I need to make time."

"I've been waiting for your call," Javier said. "Anything I can do to help, I will."

Tuck looked at me. "Mind if I use your back room?"

I nodded. "Of course." As the two of them walked away, I said to Marcus and Rocky, "Do think I could charge the town rent for using my office as a police substation?"

Marcus laughed. "Might be worth the ask."

I HAD ALMOST FORGOTTEN that Javier and Tuck were in the back when they finally emerged. I wouldn't say they looked like buddies, but any hostility that had lingered on Petra's shoulders was gone. He apologized again as he headed toward the door, and then he looked back and said, "Santa's coming again starting tomorrow?"

"He is," I said and tried not to cringe as he responded.

"Maybe I'll bring my boys."

"Oh, that would be great. Please do."

He smiled and started his walk back to the door as Cynthia, the nurse from the hospital who had acted a little weird about Bixley, walked in. The two stopped and stared at one another, and for a moment, I thought I heard that whistling sound that always rings across the scene when there's about to be a shoot-out in an old Western. Clearly, there was no love lost between these two.

"Nurse Delilah. Why are you here?"

The nurse craned her neck back and said, "Excuse me. Last I checked this was a public institution." She leaned around Javier and caught my eye. "You're open right?"

"We are. In fact, we'd love for you to come in." Out of the corner of my eye I saw Tuck watching me, and I took out my phone to text him. "She knew Bixley. Well."

He gave me a quick nod as he glanced at his own phone and then played it cool. At least I guessed that's what he was doing as he began fervently studying the sex book section. If I hadn't been concerned about the confrontation mounting at the entrance to my store, I would have snapped a picture.

"The nice woman who runs this store doesn't need the likes of you in here, Nurse Delilah." Petra's voice was shaking with rage, and his hands were balled into fists by his side.

Now, that's a real about-face in the course of a half-hour, I thought. From attacker to protector. That whiplash might hurt later. Still, I didn't really need protecting from my own customers. I stepped forward and said, "Javier, what's all this about? Cynthia is welcome in my store."

"You want to let a murderer in here?" Javier spat.

"Wait, what, whoa! A murderer?"

Cynthia's face had gone ice cold, and when she spoke it was in a jagged whisper. "I. Am. Not. A. Murderer."

"Well, if not, then you worked with one, maybe helped him. Let him keep doing what he was doing," Javier stepped closer to Cynthia, and I was glad to see both Tuck and Marcus moving forward.

"Javier, what is going on here?" Tuck asked, a "how to talk to your kids about sex" book under his arm.

"This woman was Bixley's assistant. She helped him murder my father and all those other people, too. You need to arrest her, Sheriff." Javier's voice was thick with anger and tears.

"That's a pretty serious accusation you're lobbing at . . . ," he stopped and looked Cynthia. "I'm sorry. Your name?"

"I'm not telling you my name, not after an accusation like that. You need to arrest him for slander." Her volume level was rising, and now, a small crowd was gathering both in the store and outside.

"Ma'am, I'm not accusing you of anything. I'm just trying to get at the heart of a murder." Tuck took off his hat and slowed his voice as he approached Cynthia.

But she wasn't haven't any of it. "I'm sorry, Sheriff. But you don't know me, and I certainly don't know you. I will have my attorney contact you." Cynthia looked at me. "I'm sorry for the scene, Harvey, but this is too big for me to take any risks." Her voice grew softer. "I hope you understand."

With that, she turned and walked out the door, and while I appreciated her apology – even though she hadn't needed to give it – I didn't understand, not at all. This wasn't some legal TV show where everyone called their attorneys for everything. This was St. Marin's, our quiet town, and that was Tuck Mason, a good sheriff and a great man. I had no idea why Cynthia was so defensive, but I had a feeling she hadn't done herself any favors with that reaction. She sounded like she had something to hide, and that could be a dangerous position to take in a murder investigation.

Tuck looked at me with his eyebrows raised and tilted his

head toward the café before turning to Javier and saying, "Mr. Petra, have a minute?"

Javier shrugged and followed the sheriff toward a table. I scooted along behind, so curious that my ribs were tingling with anticipation. Someday I might get bored of trying to find the answers to, well, anything – including murder, but today was not that day.

As we sat down, Rocky brought us a carafe of coffee, three mugs, and cream and sugar, and I smiled in a way that I hoped gave her the "I'll tell you later" signal as I sat down.

We took a couple of moments to dress our coffee – me with extra sugar and enough cream to make it an almost-latte – and then Tuck said, "Okay, Mr. Petra, what was that about?"

Javier took a long draw from his mug and then said, "She was always around when Bixley was. I almost never saw him if I didn't see her, too. She was there the night my dad was killed, too." His voice was quiet, but I could feel the tension ratcheting up as he spoke.

"So you suspected her of working with Bixley to do what, exactly?" Tuck's question was cautious. I had no doubt he knew exactly what Javier suspected, but he wasn't about to reveal anything, especially not about a potential serial killer.

"To murder people, sheriff." Javier's eyebrows furrowed. "I know you've heard the talk. Bixley was killing people who he felt had lived too long, who he thought would be 'better off' on the other side."

"Do you have any proof of that, Mr. Petra?" Tuck's voice was, again, neutral, but I could tell by the tiny tightness in the corner of his eyes that he hoped Javier did have something, anything, to help him figure out what Bixley had been doing and why someone wanted to kill him.

"I'm not sure." Javier looked down at his hands. "I stole a vial of my father's blood the day before he died. He was getting weak so fast, and it just didn't seem right." He looked up at met my eyes. "I mean, he was definitely dying, but this seemed different. Like, he'd never had a cough before, but now he did."

Tuck took out his notebook and jotted something down. "So his symptoms changed?"

Javier nodded vigorously. "Yes, exactly. If he was sick from cancer, I expected the symptoms would stay largely the same as each time, only worse. But he'd never coughed before. Never complained of stomach pain either."

"Could the cancer have spread to his stomach?" I asked, not sure how cancer worked exactly but confident that it did spread if not treated.

"Not according to his last CAT scan, no." Javier's voice was firm. "No, this was just different. So when the nurse took his blood, I took a vial." He sucked a breath through his teeth. "Was that illegal?"

"I'm not sure, so I'm going to pretend you didn't ask me that question," Tuck said. "Do you still have the vial?"

"Right here." He patted the breast pocket of his plaid, button-down shirt. "I didn't want to lose it, but I hadn't figured out how to get it tested." He sighed. "I didn't even really know what to test it for."

I put out my hand after getting a quick nod of approval from Tuck. "I can get this taken care of, Javier. Discreetly. We'll know tomorrow whether there was something amiss about your father's bloodwork." Javier handed me the vial.

Tuck stood. "Until then, Mr. Petra, no more threats, okay? Let's not show our hand until we know what we've been dealt."

Javier let out a long slow breath. "Thank you. You're the first people who have really listened, well, besides Danita." His shoulders slumped. "You're looking into her murder, too?"

"Oh, I look into every murder, Mr. Petra. And hers has my special focus for the rest of the day." He put a hand on Javier's shoulder. "I'll be in touch once we get the results of the blood work."

Javier shook Tuck's hand and gave me a small smile before turning and leaving the shop.

"I can't ask him, Harvey. Just in case there are legal questions about that blood, but ask Bear to rush it, will you?" Tuck said quietly as I scooted beside him to the door.

"You got it," I said as I wrapped my fingers around the blood of a man who also might have been murdered.

BEAR CAME AS SOON as I texted and picked up the vial. He didn't ask questions beyond what I was looking for, and all I could tell him was that the patient had had cancer but that he'd started coughing and complaining of stomach pain that seemed out of the ordinary.

"That's enough to go on. I'll get a full panel worked up on rush. Have you some results in the morning." Bear hugged me.

12

W ednesday is that day of the week that I usually feel myself waning. The big joy of new book releases on Tuesday has passed, and we're not into the weekend burst of sales. So I often take Wednesdays and do some maintenance for the store – check our inventory, plan a new window display, look at what book event I could schedule.

So that's what I did. I ordered books, and I planned a snow-related window display for after the holidays. I was eager to feature Billy Coffey's *Snow Day* since I'd just come across his work and was loving the sort of supernatural timbre and mountain folklore of his stories. Then, I decided to see if I could get him to come read for us in the new year and was delighted when he immediately replied to my email and said yes.

Between those tasks and chatting with customers who stopped by my throne, where I'd added a lap blanket, a side table, and a foot stool just to completely own my incapacitated status, I totally forgot to check the ticket sales for the John Green event until late afternoon. And when I did, I let out a loud whoop and got stares from customers and employees alike.

Tiffany trotted over – the woman ran everywhere – and said, "So what brings about that shout of delight?"

I was fairly bouncing in my thoroughly padded seat. "We've sold out for the Green event already. I can't believe it."

"Are you kidding? I'm not that much of a reader," she blushed, "No offense – and even I know John Green's books. Plus, do you know how many teenagers just begged their parents for an early Hanukkah or Christmas present? I'm not surprised at all."

"Well, when you put it that way . . ." I stood up and stretched. "Still, that's a huge relief. That means we'll have a big donation to give to hospice just from the ticket sales, and anything we make in book sales will be bonus."

"Speaking of which," Marcus said as he toted a huge box from the back room. " The books are here."

My stomach suddenly plummeted, and then I felt a rush of relief. I had totally forgotten about the books – I mean, I'd ordered them, but with all the events of the past few days, I had totally forgotten to check on the delivery status. Thank goodness they'd arrived. I sat back down as the waves of anxiety passed into peace of mind.

"What do you think we should do with them, Marcus?" I asked because I couldn't even begin to formulate a plan just then.

He tossed the box in the air like it was full of marshmallows and said, "Well, what do you think of doing a big four-sided Christmas tree of books right in the front of the store?"

"I love that idea, but isn't that a lot of work since we need to take a bunch of the books to the high school for Green to sign Saturday night?"

"That's why we made this," Rocky said as she came out from behind her café counter with what looked like a cardboard M.C. Escher sculpture. "It means you don't have to use many books to display them festively."

I eyed the cardboard and then shook my head. "I'm sorry. I can't ever picture things like this. Can you show me?"

"Give us ten minutes," Rocky said and bustled her way to the front of the store with her cardboard cutout.

"You know what they're up to?" I asked Tiffany as she watched Marcus pick up two more boxes and carry all of them to the front with nary a waddle.

"Not a clue, but I'm dying to find out." She jogged to the front of the shop, and I leaned my head back and shut my eyes. I really needed some caffeine, but if I drank it now, I'd be up all night. So I opted for a quick rest.

A quick rest that ended when Damien woke me up by asking, "Do you always drool?"

I shot to my feet and then immediately groaned as the ache in my ankle reached my head. "Darn it." I gave my head a little shake and then focused on Damien's face in front of me. He had his Santa beard hanging below his chin, so he looked like a black, super-elderly member of ZZ Top. "Did I sleep that long?" I looked up at the clock – only five.

"Nope, I came in early. Thought maybe I could help out some. You know, spiff up Santa's sleigh and such." He held up an armload of the tackiest gold garland I had ever seen.

"You're not putting that on the sleigh," I said as I shifted my scooter under my leg and started to make my way to see what Rocky and Marcus had created.

"Why not?" Damien said in a tone that was only slightly less than a whine. "It's gold."

"Yes, I can see that. It is also ugly. Thanks for the offer, but I think Santa's sleigh looks great as is." I stopped short when I saw that right next to said sleigh, Marcus and Rocky had created a beautiful tree that shifted from gold to aqua to green and back to off-white in just such a way that it looked perfectly like Christmas. "Oh, guys, this looks amazing. Wow."

Marcus stepped back. "You like it?"

"I love it. It's perfect." I scooted a little closer. "And it's only two copies on each tier? Wow."

"Yep, so you see the books, and you can pick them up easily, but it doesn't take our full inventory to create the effect." Rocky was fairly beaming. "I saw something like it on Pinterest and wanted to try it out."

"Well, anytime you want to create something for my shop, you have my blanket permission." I noticed that behind the sleigh, Marcus and Rocky had stacked extra copies of each title so that we could keep the tree fresh. "Another task for our elf?"

"Exactly," Marcus said. "Easy enough. When they return from helping a kid sit with Santa, they can grab any books we need."

Damien sighed. "There we go again. Santa's labor being stolen for the man."

I looked at the not-quite Santa and said, "Seriously? Why doesn't Santa go wait in the back until it's show time? We don't want to give away the show with you out here in your Nikes and no beard."

Marcus looked at Damien's shoes. "Nice Airs." The two men walked into the back room talking about Air Jordans like I might talk about first editions of Margaret Atwood's *The Cat's Eye*.

A few minutes later, Marcus returned with a couple more boxes of books to finish out the display and supply the back-stock table, and I headed to the back room to grab the dinner I'd packed and to take a break before the Santa rush began. The conversation on Instagram hadn't slowed down since Damien's original post, especially since he kept feeding the fire with more sexy Santa selfies, and I thought our crowd might be big. I was just glad it was a school night because then at least the children wouldn't have to mingle with the folks hoping to date Santa.

Damien was lounging on the loveseat in the corner, and I could see he was checking out his likes on Insta. I thought it might be wise to slow his roll a little with the fandom, help him get in the mood to be Santa a little, so I decided to take one for the St. Marin's community and make small talk. "Damien, what did you do for Christmas as a kid? Did you go sit on Santa's lap somewhere?"

He sat up and smiled. "Actually, yeah. My dad brought me right here to this spot every year. He said it was a place I needed to know, and he told me all about when it was a gas station, about all the famous folks who stopped here because it was in the *Green Book*."

I remembered when I'd learned all that history about my store, about the years it was the only place black people could stop in St. Marin's. The plaque by the door helped remind people of that history, and I was proud to be a small part of it. "So going to see Santa was special. I can see why you wanted the job."

"Yeah," his voice grew wistful. "Dad worked a lot, so anytime I got to do something with just him, it was special. Mom wasn't so keen on Santa, thought it was teaching me to believe in lies, I guess, but Dad always said it was about magic. 'Magic is real, son. Never forget it.'"

For a minute, I thought I saw a tear in Damien's eye, but he turned away and cleared his throat. "Those memories are extra special now."

I sighed. "Your dad is no longer with us?"

"Died two months ago. He had Alzheimer's, early onset kind. He still knew me though. Knew my sister, too." Damien's voice got very soft. "Died just before he got to meet my niece, his first grandchild."

I got up from the table where I'd been picking at my stew

and hopped over to sit next to Damien. I wanted to hug him, but I didn't think he'd take kindly. "I'm so sorry. That's awful."

"Yeah, yeah it is." He took a deep breath and then stood up. "Mind if I get into character early. I can just wave to people if you want."

I glanced at the clock on the wall. Just short of six. "No, it's fine. Go ahead and get started. It might be slow since we didn't advertise you'd be here until six thirty, but feel free to get going. I'll make a note to pay you for the hours."

He smiled then and bent down to hug me. "Thanks, Harvey."

I stiffened in surprise but then patted him on the back. "No problem, Damien. Your dad would be proud."

A cloud passed over his face. "I hope so." Then the sly smile popped back up on his cheeks, and he swaggered out after putting his beard in place and slipping his boots over his Nikes.

I shook my head with a laugh. What an odd Santa he was.

THE LINE for Santa was steady if, as I expected, a bit older than our intended demographic. The amount of giggling was about the same as the previous nights, though, so I took it as a win. Book sales weren't that brisk, but Rocky's mulled cider and holiday-themed lattes were a hit. I figured that was just fine because word of mouth about good coffee was just about as effective as word of mouth about good books. Surely everyone had at least one book-loving friend, and my hope is that the copious number of Instagram photos and TikTok videos that were being taken would reach those readers better than any newspaper campaign.

After I shooed the last few flirtatious young women away from the sleigh and thanked Damien for a good night's work, Mayhem and I closed up shop and enjoyed the quiet walk home. This time, I hadn't even had to cajole my friends into letting me leave on my own, thank goodness. Apparently, they trusted me, at least a little, and it seemed they trusted the town to protect me, too. It was one of my favorite things about life in a small town: everywhere, even home, was close enough to reach in even the coldest weather.

THE NEXT MORNING, I got to the store bright and early, eager to replenish the John Green tree, which had been a steady seller even to Damien's fan club. I had just opened the door and was turning to lock it behind me when Tuck popped into the window with his hand over his eyes to help him see past the early morning glare on the glass.

I swung the door open and said, "Looking for me."

He stepped back with a gasp and said, "Yes, um, yes I was." He put his hand on his chest. "Sorry, you scared me."

I laughed. "Got the jump on you, huh?"

He shook his head and gave me a bit of side eye. "I suppose. Have a minute?"

"Sure. Let me start a pot of coffee, and then we can sit in the fiction section." I looked out the window. People were just starting to make their way onto Main Street, but I wasn't ready for customers yet. "The back room is a little too dark for me this bright and sunny morning, and I don't really want to have customers just yet."

"Makes sense to me," the sheriff said as he scooped a copy of *Turtles All The Way Down* off the Green Christmas tree and headed deeper into the store.

A few moments later, I balanced two steaming cups of coffee on my scooter, a new skill I had acquired, to our wing-back chairs and handed my friend his. He took it without looking up from the page and read for a second more before saying, "This guy is good. Have you read this?"

I smiled. "I have. I've read all of his book actually. I didn't peg you for a YA fiction type, though."

"What? You think I'd read only true crime or something," he said with a smile.

"Actually, I was thinking Saul Bellow might be more your speed. Or Randall Kenan. Maybe Wallace Stegner."

"So you think I'm an atmospheric, methodical person who appreciates subtle detail rather than big action?"

My jaw dropped open. "Well, yes, now that you say it. I do." I loved that about Tuck. He was a jokester, and a fine police officer. But he always surprised me, too. I wasn't surprised, mind you, that he was well-read, just that he was that thoughtful about his own reading tastes. Most people weren't.

"I take that as a fine compliment, Harvey Beckett. But now, well, I have to get to something more fast-paced, I'm afraid. I have the findings from Danita's autopsy."

I sat forward. "And?"

"Want to guess?"

"Not really. Insulin poisoning again?"

Tuck nodded. "Seems we have a rash of murders all committed the same way."

"That can't be a coincidence." I sat back and looked at my cast. Ollie's crying Santa was still the perfect portrayal of how this holiday season was turning out. Still beautiful and lit with joy but also so sorrowful, too.

"No, it can't. But listen, Harvey, I'm only telling you this because you have, somehow, ended up with connections to everyone involved. I wanted you to have the full story because – and hear me now – I didn't want you trying to dig anything up on your own. No sleuthing." His face was very serious, and I knew he meant what he said.

"No sleuthing. I'm not exactly subtle at the moment, if you haven't noticed." I pointed toward the cast and the scooter.

"What do you mean 'at the moment?'" Tuck said with a wink. "I don't think subtlety is your specialty."

"Touché," I said with a laugh as he stood. "Seriously, though, I just really want all this sorted so we can go back to pretending like we live in a movie and enjoy the holidays. But I will gladly let you sort it. I'm going to sit right here and enjoy this coffee."

"Good plan, Ms. Beckett." Tuck drained his mug and dropped it in the café sink before he headed out.

I SPENT the next hour or so refilling displays and facing out titles on shelves. I really needed to get more books down from our overstock shelves that Woody had installed earlier in the year, but there was no way I was trying to climb the library ladders with this cast. So I made a note to ask Marcus to help me out with that when he came in.

Soon, Rocky joined me, and I could hear the espresso grinder going as I tidied up the front register and got ready to open the shop. It was one of my favorite moments of the day – the minutes before the first customer came in. Everything felt full of potential.

I was just heading to turn on the open sign when I noticed Cynthia Delilah outside on the sidewalk. She kept looking at her watch and then the bookstore's front door in the age old, "When will this store open already?" stance. I glanced at my own watch and saw I had a few minutes before ten. So I left the sign off and cracked open the door.

"Cynthia, do you need something?" I asked, keeping the door closed firmly around everything but my face.

"Oh, hi, Harvey. I was hoping to talk to you for a few minutes before it got too busy. Do you mind?"

I ran through all the possible problems with letting her in and decided that in broad daylight with Rocky in the room, even I and my cast could handle an angry thirty-something woman. And she didn't seem that angry this morning. In fact, she looked pretty sad.

"Sure. Come in," I said as I scooted back and let her through the door. I didn't lock it behind her, trusting the universe to bring me customers if I needed the presence of more people for some reason. Past experience had taught me not to be alone, if I could help it, with anyone suspected of a violent crime.

I headed right for my throne, but I gestured toward the folding chair that Marcus had stationed nearby for customers who wanted to "set a spell," as my grandmother would have said, to talk. Cynthia pulled it over and sat down heavily.

"Thanks for letting me in, Harvey. I know I didn't make the best impression the other day." A flush of color spread up her temples.

"Well, I'm not going to lie. Invoking a lawyer probably wasn't the most casual move in the book." I smiled and found that I genuinely felt warmth for this woman who had, several times, seemed a bit intimidating to me.

"I know. I just panicked. His accusation took me by surprise." She met my gaze. "I wouldn't hurt anyone, Harvey. For whatever reason, I need you to know that."

I nodded. I understood. I hated when people thought the worst of me, even when I deserved it. "I hear you, but Javier seemed so sure of what he was saying."

She let out a long, thin breath and slid her fingers into her braids as she looked up at the ceiling. "He's sure because he's right. I was with Bixley a lot."

My eyes grew wide, and I wanted to either ask a thousand questions or scoot as fast as I could to Rocky's side. But I stayed put and waited. Silence brought about a lot of information if you let it linger.

After a few seconds, Cynthia met my gaze. "I was trying to

stop him, Harvey. I was trying to keep him from killing anyone else."

Her words dropped like lead into the space between us, and I just stared at her for a moment before I could find my voice again. "Are you saying you knew Bixley was killing patients?"

She nodded. "I did, but I couldn't prove it. I did everything I could to catch him red-handed. See him slip the syringe into an IV line, find the empty insulin containers, something. But he was too good. I couldn't find anything."

I frowned. "So why not just tell Tuck that the other day?"

"Like I said, I panicked. I worried that since I couldn't prove Bixley did it, then I couldn't prove I didn't. And if Javier had noticed how I was always with Bixley, then I had to assume that other people did, too." She wrung her hands in her lap. "But now Danita . . ."

"Now someone else has died, someone innocent, and you feel guilty?" I caught her gaze and held it.

"Yes. I know I need to go to the sheriff, but I'm scared. I thought if maybe I told you first, and if you believed me, I'd have the courage to tell him." Her eyes dropped to her lap.

I let out a long, slow breath. "First, I do believe you, and while I can't speak for the sheriff, I think he'll believe you, too."

She looked up then, and I saw a little spark of hope hit her eyes.

"But secondly, I need you to understand something. You did nothing wrong, Cynthia. If what you are telling me is true – and I believe it is – then you did all you could. You are not responsible for Bixley's actions. He is. You did your best to stop him, which is admirable, but it is not your fault those people died." I had lived a lot of years feeling guilty for the things other people I'd known had done, and I'd bent myself to make space for that guilt in my life rather than letting them carry it. I didn't want to see Cynthia have to bend that way, too.

I saw Cynthia set her jaw, and she drew in a shuddering

breath. "I'll try to believe you about that." She stood up. "Okay, I'm ready. The sheriff will probably be in his office by now, right?"

"I expect so." I stood up with her. "If you want to wait until Marcus comes in, I'll go with you."

She reached over and squeezed my hand. "Thank you, Harvey. That means a lot, but this thing, I need to do this now and on my own."

I leaned over and hugged her. "Let me know how it goes?"

She nodded and went out the door. I grabbed my phone and texted Tuck. "You at the station?"

"Yep, just finishing my second cup. Why?"

"Cynthia Delilah is on her way to you. You need to hear what she has to say."

An eyeroll emoji came through next. "You just can't help yourself can you," the sheriff's next text said.

"This time, the clue came to me."

13

D aniel popped his head around the corner of the religion section just before noon and found me knee-deep in a real alphabetization project. I needed time to think about what Cynthia had said and to figure out what was needling me about the murders Bixley had, still allegedly but more and more surely, committed. Putting things in alphabetical order required just enough of my focus to free up the rest of my mind to ponder.

But still, an hour into my project, I wasn't any closer to figuring out what was going on. I knew all these murders were connected – Mr. Petra, Bixley, Danita – but I just couldn't see how. Clearly, insulin poisoning was significant, but I couldn't tell why. At least not yet.

So when Daniel turned up with an offer to take me and the dogs to Lu's truck for carnitas tacos, I jumped at the chance to get away, take in some fresh air, and run my thoughts by him. Sometimes the only way I sorted out my own brain was by talking, and Daniel was the best listener I knew.

Mayhem and Taco were in rare and well-behaved form as we walked. They only sniffed briefly, and they didn't try to dislocate Daniel's shoulder by tugging, which was good because I was holding onto his other arm and didn't think I'd stay upright if I was pulled ahead at too quick a clip. We reached the taco truck, and Daniel tied the dogs to a lamp post while he and I sat down and scarfed our hot food in the cold air.

Between bites, I told Daniel about Cynthia and the findings from Danita's autopsy. I'd already filled him in about Mr. Petra's blood work, and of course everyone knew Bixley's cause of death. "You'd think this much insulin going missing would raise an eyebrow or two?"

Daniel nodded. "You'd think, unless the killer has their own supply."

"True. I guess that's possible, but Bixley – where did he get his? The logical place would be the hospital, but wouldn't someone notice? I don't know how much insulin it takes to kill a person, but I'd think it's a lot. And if he killed multiple people?"

"Hold that thought." Daniel got up and returned to Lu's truck, coming back a moment later with two piping hot churros that made the world smell like paradise. "Maybe he was doctoring files or something, changing up the charts of people who needed the insulin to make it look like they needed more than they actually took?"

I munched on my crunchy, cinnamon stick of delight and pondered. "That's probably a question for Bear, huh?"

"Better yet," Daniel said. "Why not suggest Tuck – you know the man paid to investigate things – look into it?"

I sighed. "You're right." I sighed again and took out my phone. I texted Tuck with my questions, and then tucked the phone back in my pocket.

Daniel squeezed my shoulders and then succeeded in shoving two-thirds of a churro in his mouth at one time.

"I know, I know," I said with a laugh. "You didn't want it to get cold."

He nodded vigorously as he struggled to chew.

"Well, while you're occupied, let me tell you about some of Damien's visitors last night." I spent the next few minutes regaling my fiancé about the various ways girls had flirted with our Santa, including the one young woman who had faked a fall in front of him just so that he'd have to help her up. "I guess he couldn't see the big wink she threw her friends before she launched herself against the sleigh."

Daniel let out a low groan, and it took me a minute to realize he was reacting to my story not to the immense amount of food he had consumed.

"Now, come on. You mean to tell me if I hadn't wooed you with my womanish charms and my hound dog, you wouldn't have, er, fallen for me if I fell for you." I waggled my eyebrows.

"The problem with that scenario, Ms. Beckett, is that you would have really fallen, probably broken a wrist, and been unconscious as I fell in love at first sight." He smiled and pulled me closer.

"True enough." I sat quietly for a few moments and enjoyed the chance to people watch. A middle-aged man and a young boy who I took to be his son were walking along and looking in the windows of the stores. They looked happy, content, and I thought back to Damien's story about his father and how sad it must have been for everyone that he didn't live to see his first grandchild. "It was all a bit ridiculous with Studly Santa, I'll grant you, but I think Damien kind of needed the pick-me-up."

I told Daniel about Damien's father and how sad the young man had looked as he'd recounted the story. Daniel said, "That is a shame." He let out a long sigh as he watched a miniature Yorkshire Terrier try to lift its leg high enough to pee on the bottom of a lamp post. "How long ago was that?"

I thought a moment and tried to remember if Damien had

told me. "You know, I don't know. I'm not sure he said. Seemed recent though." I stood and resisted the urge to press my luck and try to pull Daniel up beside me. He was right. I could injure myself again at any moment.

As we walked back to the shop, I thought about my parents, how lucky I was to still have them both with me – both in the fact that they were alive and that they were, at this moment, standing at the doorway of my shop admiring Marcus's Christmas tree.

Daniel greeted them, said he looked forward to dinner later, and kissed me on the cheek before heading back to his garage. Thursday nights had become a sort of family night. We ordered carry-out on a rotating basis so that once a month or so Dad got to bring in brisket, French fries, and hush puppies and Mom couldn't complain. We usually ate at their condo, and their dog Benji got to party down on the leftovers. Tonight, though, given my injury and the two flights of stairs between the car and my parents' house, we were settling in at my place, Benji included. Fortunately, Mart had tidied up the night before because by the time I got home from work each night this week, I'd been too tired to do anything but drop onto the couch for some mindless TV. My mom would have a fit if she saw I took my pants off in the living room not once, but twice. It was brisket night, though, so I might have gotten away with my slovenliness since Mom was sure to be trying to curtail Dad's intake of slow-cooked beef.

BY THE TIME dinner rolled around, I was again exhausted – scooting was far more tiring than walking – but I did resist the urge to slither out of my dress pants in the living room, but only just barely. I only stayed out of pjs because I'd worn jeans to work that day. If it had been dress pants, my parents might have seen more of me than they'd seen since I was five.

Mom and Dad had let themselves in already, and so the house was filled with the scent of spices and fried bread. It smelled like comfort, and I was all in. Mart was joining us tonight because, well, this was her house, too, and I was glad. Mart was every bit my mom's favorite, especially since Mart had begun giving Mom bottles of wine on the regular since she got so many and we didn't want to kill our livers. When I came in, Mart and Mom were on the couch, a bottle of wine on the coffee table and three glasses out, two already full. Mom filled mine before I even sat down, and I took a sip of a big, heady zinfandel that had hints of pepper. The fact that I thought of wine and pepper in the same moment told me I'd talked too much wine with Mart.

Daniel arrived a few minutes after me, and Mayhem, Taco, and Benji did a quick sniff and greet before collapsing on the veritable den of dog beds by the blazing fire. Within moments, three distinct snores rose from the cushions, and Aslan looked first at me and then at them as if to say, "Despicable creatures. I would never" before she curled into a ball and began her usual wheeze-breathing against her left paw.

Dad poured Daniel a beer in a chilled mug, and it was only then that I realized my parents had been here, well, long enough to chill a mug. "When did you guys get here?"

Dad looked at Mom, and she looked away. I knew then, something was going on. "Oh, just a bit ago," Dad said.

I sighed and caught Daniel's eye. He shrugged and looked away, and then, I knew he was in on it.

Next, I turned to Mart, and she smiled. It was an easy smile. Natural, even, which told me I was the only one not in the know.

"Okay, someone spill it. What's going on?" My stomach was dancing, and I couldn't tell if I was excited about the prospect of something amazing or terrified that this surprise might be terrible.

Mom looked at Dad, who looked at Daniel, who looked at Mart, and I followed the train of questions about who would tell me. Then I started to stand as Mom said, "John Green is coming to dinner tomorrow night."

I dropped back into my chair and looked from one face to the other, hoping something in these faces I loved would translate that news into language I could understand. Mart must have seen my confusion because she moved over and sat on the arm of my chair. "Harvey, your mom and dad invited John Green to have dinner with us here at our house tomorrow night, and he said yes."

Suddenly, the words jolted into place in my head, and I squawked, "What?!" I put my hands against my chest and again wondered if I was feeling excited or terrified. My heart was leaping, so maybe it was both. "Here? With us? In our house? What?!"

Daniel knelt down in front of me, and I took a deep breath. "Yes, here, with all of us, Henri and Bear, and Tuck and Lu. Your mom called his publicist and invited him. Apparently, he's coming into town early to enjoy a weekend away, so he said he'd be delighted to have a home-cooked meal."

Panic set in full-scale then as the idea of having to cook for nine people while I was on a scooter, had a major event the following day, and still needed to manage my bookstore hit me. I started to have a little trouble breathing until Daniel caught my eye again. "Breathe, Harvey. Your parents came early today and cleaned, and they'll be here to manage the house tomorrow afternoon. I'm still picking Mr. Green up from the airport, and Mart will be here to help Lu with the food. You don't have to do anything except come home, be yourself, and eat tamales. Everything else is taken care of."

My eyes still felt like they might pop out of my head, but I was feeling oxygen reach my brain again and began to breath more slowly. "Okay. Okay," I said. "But what about the store? I mean, I feel bad leaving Marcus to manage The Swaggering Santa tonight, and I don't want to ask him to do it two nights in a row."

Dad walked over and handed me my glass of wine. "Marcus is fine to take care of the store tomorrow night, and Tiffany will be there, too. Stephen and Walter also offered to help out as elves, so there's nothing to worry about, Sweetheart," Dad said.

I pictured Stephen and Walter in elf costumes and immediately conjured a vision of David Sedaris as an elf in *Santaland Diaries* and started to laugh. My two gay friends dressed as elves just like one of the most famous gay authors in the world. It was too spot-on to be casual, and so I had to ask. "Really as elves, or was that just as figure of speech?" I could barely get the question out I was laughing so hard.

"Oh no, they have outfits," Mart said. "They are thinking what I know you are thinking. Galen has promised to come by and photograph things in the hopes that Sedaris himself might see the photos."

Then, I completely lost it. The idea of my friends as elves being seen on social media by David Sedaris. John Green being in my house for dinner. It was all so amazing that I could not stop laughing.

So my friends and parents helped me to my feet, rolled me to the table, and piled my plate with brisket until I was forced to eat instead of laugh.

After my belly was full and my giggles curtailed, I started thinking about the next night, and my nerves returned. "I can't sustain an entire evening's conversation with one of my favorite authors. I'll be too self-conscious. I don't want to say something stupid, compliment some book that only a dolt would read, or something."

Mart rolled her eyes. "Harvey, you are the first person in the world to say no book is beneath anyone, so why would you be worried about that? And you can talk books for hours."

"Plus," Mom added with nonchalance, "we won't be here all evening anyway. John wants to see your store after dinner."

I choked on my pumpkin pie. "What?!"

Daniel patted my hand. "Are you choking because one of your favorite authors wants to see your store or because your mom is calling one of your favorite authors by his first name?"

Mom said, "Oh pish."

I laughed. "Both, I think. Really – he wants to see my store?"

"Said he wouldn't miss it," Dad said.

I puffed up my cheeks and let out a sputter of breath. "Guess I'll be doing a major cleaning tomorrow."

"Already got that covered," Mom said. "Elle, Cate, Lucas, and Woody are coming in the morning when you open. You tell them what needs doing, and they'll do it."

I sat back in my chair and looked at these four amazing people around me. "You guys really did think of everything, didn't you?"

"Almost," Mart said, "but we do need to find you an outfit for tomorrow."

I sighed. Fashion was never my top priority, but even I knew that a proper outfit would allay my fears about looking frumpy for this momentous day. Mart wheeled up my scooter. "To the closet," I said as I raised my hand in the air. "I will prevail."

I could hear Mom, Dad, and Daniel chuckling as they began to clean up the dishes.

THE NEXT MORNING, I put on my black dress pants and the peasant blouse that Mart had said would look both artsy and professional and slipped into my red Mary Janes. My best friend had gone so far as to lay out my jewelry, so I slipped on my rings, taking a minute to admire the topaz engagement ring Daniel had picked because he knew I didn't want a diamond, and then put on my necklace. Mart had wanted me to wear earrings, too, but since I had let my holes close up, I had to settle for the two topaz studs I wore in my left ear.

I clipped my curls down into place with the help of a little pomade and then looked in the mirror. I was surprised to see that I looked not only pulled together but also like myself. My decision to only buy and wear things I loved when I moved to St. Marin's was paying off, and I felt a little spring in my scoot as I headed toward the store, Mayhem in the lead. She was becoming quite adept at being a "scooter dog," and I contemplated having her pull me around town even when I could walk again.

The shop was already abuzz when I arrived. Rocky had recruited Elle to give the café a thorough cleaning. It was always spotless, but I knew Rocky wanted her space to shine for our special guest. And Woody was dusting, with an actual feather duster. I loved a man who wasn't afraid to do work that was traditionally considered the work of women. Cate and Lucas were hauling out hand truck after hand truck of books and moving through the shelves filling gaps and resupplying the overstock shelves as Woody dusted them.

I thought briefly of the birds who made Cinderella's dress in the Disney movie and giggled as I joined Marcus at the register. "You know, you could have come in later? You are going to be here late tonight," I said.

He shrugged. "What can I say? I didn't want to miss out on the excitement. Plus, despite the fact that we now have all hands on deck," he smiled at Tiffany as she jogged past on her way to drop her bag off in the back room, "I suspect we're going to be very busy."

"Yeah, you think the event tomorrow is going to draw that much of a crowd?" I asked as I tucked my own purse into the cabinet beneath the register.

"No, I think this is." Marcus held his phone in front of my face, and I saw John Green's image from the top of his Facebook page. I scanned down and there, right at the top, was his announcement that he would be in St. Marin's this weekend for an event tomorrow night, that he was doing an event for hospice and hoped people would donate, and that he'd be stopping by my shop this evening and would be happy to sign any books people bought.

I fell into my throne and put my hands over my eyes. "This can't be happening, can it? Did John Green just plug my shop and tell people he'd sign books while he was here?"

"Yes. Yes he did. And don't forget, he's having dinner at your house beforehand." Marcus patted me on the shoulder and then leaned down as he passed by. "Enjoy it, Harvey. You deserve it."

I looked up at the ceiling and took a deep breath. Then, I let the smile that was aching to come out burst across my face. This was unbelievable.

But by ten a.m., when I flipped on the neon sign and unlocked the door, the effects of Green's post – and all the shares and retweets and Instagram stories that had spread – was in evidence because we had a line at the door. I quickly asked Woody to help me move my throne and table to just inside the door and began answering questions about Green's visit as needed. I didn't give details because my shop couldn't handle thousands of people at one time, and I figured if Green wanted people here at a certain time, he would have said so. I just said that he was expected later in the day, that people were welcome to buy their books now and come back to see him later, and that yes, of course, they could make a donation to hospice here.

About eleven, I began to panic about our stock of books, but I had to table my worry about that when Tuck came in. Tiffany slid into my seat at the front door as Tuck and I made our way to the café to talk. He'd texted to say he wanted my opinion on something, and I'd told him to come by. "So what's up?" I asked as I swigged back my second latte of the day, anticipating that I'd need the caffeine to counteract the inevitable adrenaline crash that would come soon.

"Cynthia did come by. And her story makes sense and lines up with what Javier Petra told me." He took a sip of his coffee.

"So you believe her?" I felt a wave of relief wash over me. I had been worried that my naive desire to always think the good of people might have deluded me. '

"I do. She has every reason to lie, of course, if she was assisting Bixley, but I just don't think she was. These angels of mercy usually work alone, wanting to revel in their accomplishments solo. Plus, the means of death didn't require an assistant. One syringe was all it took."

I sighed. "I wish she had found something to incriminate Bixley."

"Me, too. It's so frustrating. All of these people suspected him, and yet he was too slick, too good to get caught." Tuck leaned back and put his hands behind his head.

"Don't they always say in movies that the killer always makes a mistake?" I grinned and squinted at my friend.

He laughed. "I'm taking away your Netflix subscription."

I was just about to tell Tuck about Green's big announcement when Woody ran over. "Sheriff, I think you need to see this."

14

The sheriff followed Woody over to Santa's Sleigh-Land (as Marcus and I had taken to calling it in a sad attempt at humor to stave off despair), and I scooted right behind. I couldn't see what Woody pointed to next to one of the runners of the sleigh until Tuck took a latex glove from his back pocket and picked it up. It was a hypodermic syringe.

I stepped back and grimaced as my jaw clenched. "What is that doing here?" I had memories of the warnings hung around Ocean Beach in San Francisco that cautions visitors about going barefoot in the sand because of spent needles. It was something I was used to there, sadly perhaps, but here, in my store – I felt myself asking the question again: "Why is that here?"

Tuck shouted a request for a plastic bag to Rocky, and she came over with one and just stared at the needle. I expected she, like me, had seen needles before, but in this setting, the sight was really creepy; unsettling in a deep way.

"You cleaned in here since last week, right?" Tuck asked me.

I dropped my chin and looked at him. "Of course. I keep a

clean store." But then I sighed, "Given my injury, though, I haven't moved the tables or the sleigh to clean around them."

"So this could have been here since Bixley was killed?" Tuck's voice was kind but firm.

I nodded. "It could have been."

Woody gave me a compassionate glance. "You saw it, Sheriff. It was right up against the runner, and given that it's mostly clear . . ."

"Oh, I know. It was easy to miss, and I'm not making any judgments here. Just trying to establish a timeline." The sheriff gestured toward the chair and a half nearby. "Sit down, Harvey, before you fall down."

I did as I was told and felt a smidge better once my heartrate returned to normal. Then, it picked back up when the anger hit. "Wait, does that mean you think whoever killed Bixley actually injected him here?" I felt rage climbing up my spine. It was one thing to have someone die here. It was entirely another to have someone killed here.

"We don't know anything, Harvey." Tuck must have seen the lava of fury threatening to explode from my ears because his voice was soft and smooth. "That is one possibility, but it's also possible that this needle is here for any number of reasons."

"Like what?" I spat. Rocky put her arm around my shoulders.

"Like a drug user dropped it? Or someone who is actually diabetic?"

"Or the killer let it fall after injecting, Bixley," I added, my voice lined with steel. "So help me, if I find out someone murdered him in my shop—"

Tuck winked at Marcus, who had joined us when I had started shouting, and said, "What? You'll murder them?"

I stopped mid-sentence, stunned, because I had been about to say that very thing. I sank back against the chair. "Well, no." I felt tears gather in my throat. "But seriously, I'm terribly sad someone died here, but for this to be a crime scene, for someone to steal the innocence of Santa like this . . ." I couldn't finish.

Marcus knelt down beside me. "It's awful, Harvey. But at least we have some evidence now, right? That's a lot more than we had this morning." He looked up at Tuck who gave a knowing nod.

"He's right, Harvey. My guess is that if – and that's a big if – this is the murder weapon, the killer didn't intend to leave it behind. And if they didn't intend to leave it behind . . ." He let his voice trail off.

"They might not have been very careful about how they touched it." I smiled tentatively.

"I guess all those crime dramas do pay off from time to time," Tuck said. "I'm off. Harvey, I will let you know if we find anything here, just to ease your mind."

"Thank you, Tuck. I really appreciate that." I sighed and looked at my friends. Cate and Lucas were still tidying, but I could see Cate checking on things in our little huddle as she loaded the bookshelves. "Well, nothing more to do about that now, and we have a celebrity author coming to town."

Marcus smiled and reconvened the cleaning and stocking efforts. I scooted to my throne and took out my computer. I'd made a mental note of the kind of needle, and I figured that at least I could confirm my suspicions that this was an insulin syringe. I knew it could be something else, but I didn't think it was. It would be far too much of a coincidence to have someone die from a needle injection *and* find a random, unrelated needle in the same week.

Cate came over and leaned over the back of my chair. "A match?" she asked, catching on quickly to my query.

I looked carefully at an image of a needle on the screen, one labeled as an insulin syringe, and they sure looked the same to me. Thin tube with lots of measurement marks and a very thin needle. The one Woody found was missing the trademark orange cap, but I figured the killer had tucked that into a pocket to make the syringe subtler.

"That needle is so tiny. It reminds me of the acupuncture needles my aunt uses in her practice. She puts them into me, and I don't even feel it," Cate said. "These are a little bigger, but still. It's possible Bixley was stuck and didn't even know it."

I sighed. "You're right. If someone was distracted," I thought back to the way Bixley was acting as he came in – like he was drunk, "or intoxicated, he might not have even noticed."

Cate rubbed my shoulders. "I hate to say it, Harvey, but your store has had its first murder on the grounds."

My head dropped into my hands, and I moaned. "Great. Just what I needed today." I felt a sharp smack on the back of my head and looked up at Cate to see her scowling.

"Come on, Harvey. This isn't great, but it's not the end of the world. At least it wasn't a gruesome death, right?"

I tried to smile. "I guess you're right." I knew Cate was bothered, at least as bothered as I was, but she was trying to help me, well, keep going, and I appreciated the effort, especially since I was having dinner with John Green in just seven hours.

So I took a deep breath, closed the browser tabs, and stood up. "Alright, I'm ready." The customers had been steady since we opened, but I had been so distracted by everything that I hadn't even noticed how steady, as in lined up to buy books steady. I looked at the Christmas Tree display of Green books and realized with a start that it was almost empty. Cate looked at my face, saw the panic rising there, and followed my gaze.

"We're on it." She put two fingers in her mouth and whistled. Lucas turned on the ladder where he was filling in the last of the open shelves with titles and caught Cate's eye. She pointed to the tree and then the boxes behind the sleigh, and he nodded. Within seconds, they were refilling the shelves while I carefully counted our remaining titles. We'd put aside a couple hundred books for the event tomorrow, and I wasn't about to break into those. But at this rate, we were going to be out of books for the store by noon.

"What are we going to do?" I asked Lucas as Cate filled in the remaining spaces on the tree.

He looked from me to the nearly empty boxes and back to me. "We'll think of something. Don't worry."

I wanted to believe him, but it felt like all I had was worry inside. "Okay," I said and tried to mean it.

I was headed toward the desk to strategize about the shortage with Marcus when the bell above the door rang, and I glanced over to see a fleet of delivery people coming through with a dozen hand trucks. The woman in the lead headed straight for the desk and caught my eye, "Are you Harvey Beckett?"

"I am," I said, "What's this?" I nodded toward the stacks of boxes the men and women were unloading near Santa's Sleigh-Land.

She took a notecard out of her back pocket and handed it to me with a smile before heading back to unload her own stack of boxes.

I stared at Marcus for a minute and then opened the card. "Dear Ms. Beckett, Mr. Green told us about the event he is doing there tomorrow, and as his publisher, we wanted to be sure you had plenty of stock for the weekend. Consider these our donation to the hospice in the area. Many of us have been served by hospice in the hardest of times, and so take these gifts as our donation to your good work for that important organization. Happy Holidays." The card was signed by fifteen or twenty people, all staff at the publishing house, I presumed.

I stared at the fifty or more boxes of books at the front of the store and started to cry with joy. There it was, even in the midst of all this awfulness, the spirit of the holidays – generosity and love all in one.

Lucas walked over, dropped an arm on my shoulders and said, "See, I told you we'd figure it out."

.

15

The rest of the day went by in a blur. We sold almost half of the stock that the publisher donated, and Tiffany, Marcus, and I ran ourselves ragged keeping up with requests for other titles, ringing up customers, and answering questions about Green's visit later in the day. Thankfully, Cate and Lucas stayed on for the day and let their staffs handle their own businesses, and Rocky's mom came by to help her in the café, or our shelves would have been bare and the latte cold.

I was elated and exhausted by the time four thirty rolled around and Mom and Dad came to pick me up for dinner. Daniel had stopped in on his way to the airport to meet Mr. Green and made me love him even more when he said he'd stayed up half the night reading *Looking for Alaska* so he'd have something to talk about with our guest on the ride.

As Mom helped me to their car waiting at the curb, I got a text from Daniel saying, "I have the package," and I laughed. This could be fun, I thought for the first time before my stomach flip-flopped again.

By the time we got to my house, Lu had the kitchen

smelling like Mexican heaven, and I couldn't help but dip my finger in her mole sauce before going back to freshen my make-up and try to tame my curls. When I got back to the kitchen, I noticed that there was an extra chair at the table. "I thought there were going to be nine of us," I said to Mart as she laughed out chips and salsa.

"Oh, right. I forgot to tell you. Galen is coming. I thought that might be nice given how much publicity he's given for this event." Then she turned and looked at me with a twisted mouth. "That's okay, right?"

I smiled. "Totally okay. Something about Green being the only one without a conversation partner was making me a little jumpy," I said. But then I had a moment of concern. "But the dogs – three of them. Does John Green like dogs?"

She looked over to where Mayhem and Taco were sprawled by the fire and let out a long breath. "Seriously? Who wouldn't love those two? And Mack? Come on – he looks like someone squished him and attached toy legs to his body. That alone is endearing." She shoved a chip in her mouth. "Besides, do you really think someone as sensitive to the world as John Green would be a dog hater?"

I laughed. "Let's hope not because if it turns out he doesn't like animals, he might just drop a little in my esteem."

As if on cue, Aslan leaped up onto the back of the couch and preened. Mart laughed. "I suppose he might like cats."

I rolled my eyes. "Someone wouldn't mind that, I think." I petted the chubby black and white feline and let out one little squeal as I saw Daniel step out of his truck. They were here.

DINNER WAS DELIGHTFUL. Green was witty and fun, and he listened to our stories about how we loved his books as if we were the first people on earth to say such things. Also, he's totally a dog guy. His beloved Willie had died a couple of years earlier, and when he talked about him, I could see the sadness. But that didn't slow him down from totally getting into the dog puddle by the fire for a few minutes before we headed to the shop.

By the time we got there, the crowd was pretty thin. Some parents and children were in line to see Santa, and a few die-hard fans had held out all day. But mostly it was just the normal crowd from Friday night – a few college students with coffee and a stack of books they wouldn't buy (a practice I encouraged because I had loved it so much when I was in college), some couples on dates, and a few townsfolk who just visited the shop to find books. Green signed a few autographs, and we sold more of his books. He asked for a photo of himself with Marcus and Rocky by their Christmas tree display and promptly put it on his Instagram account, with my permission, as if he needed it.

While Marcus gave him the full tour, I did take a minute to check our supply of his books – especially given his new social media shout out – and I was glad to see we still had plenty because tomorrow was bound to be wild with Green fans.

After a tour and a short spurt of signing more books, a thing he volunteered to do for me, Green thanked us for dinner, thanked me for the tour, and told us he looked forward to the next night. I thanked him profusely, embarrassingly profusely, and watched him leave with Daniel, who was taking him to his bed and breakfast. As soon as they drove away, I collapsed into my throne and stared. "What just happened?" I said to Mom as she sat down and began rubbing my feet.

"You just lived a dream, my girl. You just lived a dream."

I nodded and let my head fall back against the seat. Yes, I had, and I was so exhilarated and so exhausted at the same time that I could barely form words. It was amazing.

. . .

BACK AT OUR HOUSE, Daniel told Mart and me that he had suggested Green visit the maritime museum and the art co-op the next day, and I was thrilled. I'd felt terrible not being able to have everyone who helped out come to dinner, even though my friends had understood, so I was glad that Daniel had talked up Cate's and Lucas's places.

"I tried to mention everyone, so I think he may come downtown, too, stop in Elle's store, maybe visit Woody's workshop, too."

I sighed. "Thank you, Daniel." I looked at Mart, "and thank you. Those bottles of wine were the special vintage from the winery, weren't they?"

Mart grinned. "Turns out my boss's daughter loves the Vlogbrothers, and so she donated for the cause. Plus, she's a big supporter of hospice, too."

"Speaking of which," Daniel said, "what's the tally on fundraising so far?"

I sat up straighter, eager to share the news that Mom had shared with me on the way home earlier. She was our financial wizard, and so she'd been keeping up with our donations. "Well, as of tonight, we're at over fifteen thousand dollars, and that's without including the book sales."

"Whoa. That seems like more than we made from ticket sales," Mart said.

"Oh yes, people have been donating directly, even if they didn't buy tickets. Mom expects we'll get some more gifts like that tomorrow, too," I added.

Mart, Daniel, and I sipped our hot chocolate and stared into the fire. I let out a long slow breath and felt the frisson of unease I'd been tamping down rise up against my collarbones. A murderer was still out there, and no matter how good my night, that fact still haunted me.

16

W hen the sun hit my eyes the next morning, I woke from a sleep so deep that it took me a minute to remember where I was. I'd been dreaming about John Green's dog Willie and the pack of pups that my friends and I had. They were a dog-scooter team, and they were in the competition for the state title. Mayhem was the lead dog, and Taco was the mascot, his legs being too short to actually run with the pack. In my dream they were just about to start the race when a green slime monster carrying a giant needle had charged into the crowd. Fortunately, Santa had stepped out to save the day, and the team went on to win the race.

It was one of those dreams that felt like it should have made me happy but actually just haunted my first minutes awake with a sense of foreboding. As I showered and opted for a sparkly headband and some careful pomading of my curls, I pondered what it could mean. I'd once heard someone say that everyone in my dreams was me, but I was having a hard time putting together exactly which version of me was the slime monster and which part was Santa.

I tried to shake off the feeling of gloom the dream had

brought along with it, and when I stepped into the kitchen, Mart's huge griddle full of bacon helped with that goal a lot. I snagged a piece from the paper towel-covered plate by the stove and sat down. Ever since we'd moved here, Mart had been cooking power breakfasts for me on the big days at the shop. It was a kindness that I was always grateful for – verbally and internally – but today more than any other day, I wanted her to know how much I appreciated her.

While she flipped the bacon, I slid a folder toward her. She looked at it, looked at me, and flipped the last few pieces before picking it up. She opened the top and then stepped backwards. "What in the world?" She met my gaze. "What is this?"

"You know what it is," I said with a smirk.

"Well, yes, since I was privileged enough to learn to read, I know what it says, but why? This is too much, Harvey? Why?" She stared at me, and I tried to keep my eyes on her, too. But the bacon was crackling, and my eyes slipped to the griddle.

She laughed and began removing pieces to the plate as I scooted over and poured us both big glasses of orange juice and prepped the toast. "It's a thank you, Mart. For everything. For moving here with me. For covering my part of the mortgage when I couldn't. But mostly just because you are amazing, the best friend I could ever have, and I wanted you to have something special. Just for you."

Mart was not a person prone to tears, but I saw one slide down her cheek before she discreetly brushed it away. "Thank you, Harvey. But this really is too much."

"You've always wanted to go there, Mart, and I knew you'd never buy yourself tickets. So now you and Symeon can eat gross-flavored jelly beans and just relax at Hogwarts."

Mart was the biggest Harry Potter fan I'd ever met, and that was saying something because as a bookstore owner, I had met people who had the lightning bolt scar *tattooed* on their forehead. So I got her and Symeon two weekend passes to Harry

Potter World. The passes were good through the next year, so I hoped she'd actually take the time off work and enjoy herself.

"Wait, you aren't coming with me?" She looked a little hurt, and I almost said, "well I could," but then a smile turned up the corner of her mouth. "He does love him some Sirius Black."

I laughed. "He would. He's a man of good taste."

Mart hugged me and then handed me a plate with six pieces of bacon. She was too good to me.

When I arrived at the store at eight, a full two hours before we were set to open, the place was already abuzz. Customers were milling around outside, hoping that Green would make another appearance, I imagined, and inside, Marcus, Rocky, and Tiffany were straightening and reshelving the disorder that lingered from the late night before.

But the biggest hullaballoo was coming from a table I had not set up or asked to be set up. Behind it, my mother was holding court with Elle, Woody, Cate, Pickle, and Daniel sitting before her with stacks of paper at hand. "What's this?" I asked as I swiped one of Daniel's papers before he could stop me.

"Support Hospice with Your Purchase or Your Gift," I read. "Mom, you had these printed? For the store?" I was feeling a little overwhelmed at Mom's thoughtfulness, but I should have realized she was going to go all out on this.

"Well, yes, some for here and some for the event tonight. There will be lots of time for people to give during the reception and beforehand."

I staggered a bit and almost lost my balance on my scooter. "What reception?" I had not heard one word about a reception.

Normally, when the bell over my shop door rings, I get excited, but this time, when it was accompanied by Max Davies's voice shouting a "Hello, Mon Chéri," I cringed.

Mom gave me a stiff smile and said, "Well, it was kind of last minute. Max offered to cater a hors d'oeuvres reception for us, and I thought it was a great idea. Give people a chance to learn a bit more about hospice and the services they offer at the end of life before Mr. Green reads."

I looked at my mom and took a deep breath. It was a good idea, but the fact that Max was doing it . . . Daniel squeezed my hand as he said, "It's for a good cause, Harvey."

My eyes shifted to his face, and he crossed his eyes and stuck out his tongue. It was the face he made when he wanted me to laugh, and it worked. I nodded. "It is. Definitely." Then I took a deep breath and turned to Max, who was looming over Daniel's shoulder, apparently waiting for my gratitude. "Thank you, Max. That's a thoughtful contribution."

Max stepped around Daniel and forced my hand from my fiancé's before taking it in his own. "I do care deeply about the cause, of course, but this gift is for you, Harvey, because you give so much."

I heard Daniel cough from somewhere near Max's rear end and hoped he wasn't getting any ideas about sticking it to his rival. But then his head poked out, and he made that face again, and I smiled. "Thank you, Max. Truly. Now, if you'll excuse me, I need to see to the store. See you tonight?" I hadn't wanted to ask, but I needed to know if I should prepare myself for an evening of this slimy adoration.

"Oh, no, I'm afraid I can't make it. I'll be managing the store. Symeon will be on site, though, to make sure things go smoothly." He took my hand to his lips again. "And of course if *you* need me, I'll be there in an instant."

I tried to smile but was sure that it came out as a grimace as I pried my hand away from Max's lips and veritably soared on my scooter into the back room. Daniel came in seconds later and helped me sit down, an assist that was necessary because I was pretty much collapsing in laughter.

"He just doesn't get it," Daniel said.

"Oh, he gets it," I added. "He just doesn't care. It's kind of sad actually, but he really thinks he can steal me away from you."

Daniel's eyes got wide, and he stuck out his bottom lip. "Should I be worried?"

I kissed that lip and said, "Well, maybe a little."

He playfully shoved me away, and my scooter sent me flying backwards into a surprisingly soft landing in a big pile of packing material that we'd been giving to customers who needed to ship gifts. Daniel rushed over, and this time he looked genuinely scared. I wasn't hurt, though, and my prat fall coming right after a visit from the man who actually caused my accident sent me into a fit of giggles so strong that I couldn't even get myself out of the bubble wrap and craft paper.

"Just leave me here and tell John," I couldn't believe he'd told me to call him John, "'thank you' for me." I let myself sink into the pile even more deeply and gave into the laughter.

A few moments later, I caught my breath and put my hands down to push myself to standing and felt something roll under my fingers. I reached down, thinking one of us had dropped a bag of pens or something into the pile by accident and came up with an entire bag of syringes just like the one Woody had found by the sleigh.

Daniel pulled me to my feet and slid my scooter under my leg. "More syringes."

I sighed. "Yep. Time to call Tuck . . . again."

"A substation here is sounding like more and more of a good idea." I nodded as I took out my phone.

TUCK ARRIVED WITHIN MINUTES, collected the bag of syringes, and headed out to do whatever he needed to do to figure out why they were there. It made no sense for those syringes to be there. After all, the murder had happened in the front of the store, and these syringes were found in a place where customers weren't allowed. But still, here they were, and that had to mean something.

What it might mean, however, was either someone who worked at my store was a killer or our killer was wily enough to slip into the back room unnoticed. When I said that to Rocky, she brought up a good point. "But why hide them there? I mean it looked like a new package. Why stash them in the back room if they are just regular insulin syringes? I'd think they aren't that hard to come by. "

I was leaning against the front register just before we were set to open, and I couldn't shake the memory of my dream with the slime monster and the thought of this package of syringes. "That's a really good question, and maybe Tuck can give us some insight on that when he comes back. Until then, we have a crowd to serve."

Rocky stood up and looked out the front windows. "Holy Moly!" She turned toward the café, "Mom, it's going to be a big one."

Rocky's mom stepped out of their small back kitchen with a tower of cinnamon rolls and said, "I think we're ready." I hoped she was right because the line at the door was down the block, and I wasn't sure I was ready.

But I flipped on the sign, unlocked the door, and smiled as a crowd streamed in with Galen and Mack leading the way with Lucas and Sasquatch close behind. Stephen and Walter came in as the crowd thinned and gave me a hug. "Thank goodness you opened the doors. We were just about out of small talk," Stephen said as he headed toward the café.

I looked from him to Walter and back again. "What's he talking about?"

"Oh, Daniel didn't tell you? He asked us to come down and warm up the line, keep them happy while they waited. So we did. It was actually really fun." He winked at me and followed his husband into the café.

I looked over at Daniel and pointed at our friends. He shrugged and smiled, and I shook my head. My people always knew just what to do to help.

I could already feel the throb building in my leg, so I scooted over to my throne where Rocky had pre-delivered a latte, Marcus had set up my laptop with the order screen, and Mom had deposited a set of flyers. Then, I started talking to the guests, beginning with my favorite customer, Galen.

"You didn't have to come, Galen. I mean, you're here enough already. I love it, but I know this isn't really your cup of tea," I smiled at him.

"If you must know, Harvey," he leaned closer from the matching wingback chair that Marcus had added next to mine, "I love John Green's books. They're just a bit off-brand for me to talk about them too much, you know."

Galen's hair was silver, but his sense of social media savvy was expert level. And he was right, of course. He was known for visiting bookstores and reviewing mysteries. So YA fiction was a bit out of his crowd's taste, and yet, he had promoted this evening's event with gusto.

"Still, thank you for all you've done. You didn't have to use so much of your pull for this event." I squeezed his hand on the arm of his chair.

He squeezed back. "I know I didn't, but hospice is such an amazing organization. I've had friends call them in for their loved ones, and they've never regretted that choice." He looked over, saw Mack comfortably puddled up with his three friends in the shop window and said, "Since I'm 'childless' for a minute, might as well shop, eh?"

I chuckled and watched him head toward the cozy mysteries. Galen was spry and healthy, but his words about his friends drove home that he was on the downhill slope of his living days. That fact made me sad, but not despondent. I'd learned, especially as Mart had been with her mom in her last days, that death is part of life, a really brutal, devastating, but fruitful, part of life if we let it be.

Mart dropped into the chair next to me, and I jolted. "Oh goodness. I didn't even see you come in."

"I used the back door. Didn't feel like having to push my way into the front." She leaned back and looked at me out of the corner of her eye. "You look thoughtful. What's up?"

I looked over at my friend and said, "Actually, I was just thinking about your mom."

She sat forward. "You were. Why is that?" Mart had told me long ago that the most painful thing about the lingering grief she felt over her mom's death was that people were afraid to talk about her. I'd done my best to always bring her up anytime she came to mind, to let Mart know I remembered her, too.

"Oh, Galen was talking about hospice, and I was thinking about how helpful the nurses and other volunteers were when your mom was sick, about how they helped us all protect her when she didn't want to keep hearing about diets or treatments or prayer when she was comfortable with her choice to not get treatment." It had been incredibly hard for Mart to watch her mom have to fend off person after person who wanted her to go to some camp for cancer patients or to just try this one more herb. Her mom had chosen her path for her last days, and still even her closest friends couldn't put aside their own sadness about what that path meant and just support her. It had been heartbreaking to watch, but hospice had been profoundly helpful about assisting Mart and her brother in setting boundaries to honor her mother's wishes.

Mart let out a long slow breath. "We are so scared to die that we can't even let people die at peace with their choice to let it happen when it comes."

I reached over and intertwined my fingers with Mart's. "We'll know better," I said.

She smiled at me. "We will." She sat up and leaned forward. "Today, though, we have a public to please and a big shindig to pull off. First things first – what are you wearing tonight?"

I sighed. I hadn't even given my outfit a second of thought, but of course, Mart had. "I have no idea. What am I wearing tonight?"

"I laid out an outfit for you – long skirt, blazer, and that headband you're wearing will go great with my mom's vintage jewelry I thought you could wear." Her voice kept getting more excited as she spoke. "I figured we'd leave here at four, and I would do your hair and make-up. I just picked up this new mascara, and I think . . ." She kept talking for a while, and I listened. But mostly I just knew I was in good hands with Mart, even as far as my mascara was concerned.

Eventually, my best friend noticed that I was glassy-eyed, I guess, because she said, "Okay. Fine. I'll stop. But four p.m., you're mine."

"Well, that doesn't sound threatening at all," I said with a smirk.

"Don't mess with me, lady, or I'll tell Max you're getting all done up for him." She laughed and bounced away to help Marcus ring up customers.

I looked out across my store and smiled.

17

A little after noon, Tuck returned with tacos and information. We slipped into the back room for a few minutes so we could eat, and he handed me a photograph. I looked down at an image of the same syringes I'd found in this very room a couple of hours before. "Okay, so you took a photo of the bag."

He jabbed at the photo with a salsa-drenched finger. "There."

I leaned down and looked at the spot next to a slice of onion. "Is that a number?"

"It is. A batch number, and this batch was ordered by the hospital about three months ago." He shoved the rest of his taco in his mouth and then wiped his face with a napkin. "And three syringes were missing from the bag."

I felt my eyes go wide. "So the syringe that killed Bixley . . ."

"Yep, part of that same batch. The killer hid the rest of the bag to keep it from being linked back to the hospital, I suspect."

I put down the rest of my taco and felt my heart sink. "So that means it was probably someone who worked at the hospital who killed Bixley?"

"Looks more and more like it. How well do you know Cynthia Delilah, Harvey?" His voice was kind but firm enough to tell me this wasn't a casual question.

"I don't know her very well at all. She's been in here a couple of times, but I haven't really talked to her much. She's your top suspect?"

Tuck rested his hands on the top of his head and looked up at the ceiling. "She has means and opportunity, maybe motive, too. It just makes sense since she worked at the hospital." The sheriff didn't look convinced, though.

"You don't think she did it though." It was more of a statement than a question.

He peeled his eyes from the ceiling and looked at me. "I don't, but I've been wrong before. It all just works if she's both Bixley's assistant and the person who killed him."

"You mean maybe she thought he was going to point the finger at her because it seemed like the board might take some action? Scapegoat her for what he did?" I had to admit that idea had some merit, but somehow, still, the idea of Cynthia as a killer wasn't sitting right with me.

"Yeah, that's what makes logical sense." He dropped his chin into his hand. "But when has murder ever been logical."

I sighed. "Right. I was just reading the latest Louise Penny mystery, and I love how Gamache goes back to the root cause of murder, to the thing that sparked the emotion that led to the actual killing."

Tuck sat up and looked at me. "That's exactly it, Harvey. I just don't see any reason beyond self-protection to kill Bixley. We know the board wasn't really interested in taking action, so even the idea that they might have feared being caught seems flimsy."

I nodded. "This may be way out there, but it also seems very personal to have killed him the way he killed his victims."

"Allegedly killed his victims."

"Right, allegedly." I made air quotes as big as my torso as I spoke. "But you know what I mean. If Cynthia was going to kill him, wouldn't she choose another method. She has medical training, after all. She could have easily used another medication – or another means altogether, cutting his brakes, for example – to get the job done. Why risk tying it back to herself so directly?"

"Yep, that's what's bugging me. This feels too neat, almost like someone is framing her. But what I don't get is the syringes back here." He gestured toward the pile of packing material I'd fallen in earlier. "You might not have found those until after the holidays if you hadn't taken another tumble."

"Hey. I've only fallen two, wait, three times in the past week." I felt a wee bit defensive about my recent accidents. "But I see what you're saying. If someone wanted to frame Cynthia, they would have left the syringes somewhere most obvious, like her car."

"Precisely." Tuck headed toward the door. " I need to talk to her again, find out more about what she might know." He stopped abruptly and looked back at me. "Just to be sure, she hasn't been back here, has she?"

I stood and thought back through the past few days. "Nope, both times she was in she was up front within my line of sight the whole time. And we keep the back door locked tight. Only Mart, Marcus, and I have keys. So no, I don't think she's been back here."

Tuck nodded and kept nodding as he walked out the door. That was a man with a lot on his mind.

After cleaning up our lunch dishes and trying, without luck, to figure out what that annoying itch about something Tuck said meant, I followed him out to the shop floor. I was stunned to see the store still packed. I had kind of forgotten that we were the "it" location on the Eastern Shore today, and the sheer number of people shopping was breathtaking.

I scooted my way back to my throne and was thrilled to see Marcus's Mom, Josie, in my seat. "Mrs. Dawson! Oh, it's good to see you," I said with an apologetic smile at the young woman to whom Josie was speaking.

Josie stood up and hugged me tight as she said, "Harvey. I hope you don't mind."

"Mind? Please do your thing." Josie wrote our monthly newsletter and did regular book reviews for us. She was in high demand for advice about books to read when a customer needed something in particular. In fact, her advice often reminded me of *Recipes for Love and Murder* by Sally Andrew, although Josie doled out more than advice on love. She was a veritable wealth of knowledge – as was her son – about books of all sorts.

I sat down quietly in the other wingback chair and made myself seem busy as I looked up our sales figures for the day so far. Really, though, I was listening as Josie recommended Flannery O'Connor's complete story collection to the young woman. "It's the best book I know for a woman who knows herself but also knows that might mean she doesn't quite fit in. O'Connor was a woman ahead of her time, and, did you know, she had a pet chicken."

"I love chickens," the young woman with red hair and a sort of 1950s look said. "Is that book here?"

Josie looked over at me, and I nodded. "Check out anthologies right over there at the end of the fiction section," I said as I pointed toward the far wall.

"Thank you," the woman said and headed toward the anthology shelf. I watched her for a couple of seconds and then turned back to Josie. "You really are spectacular at this."

Josie blushed. "Well, when you are raising a black son who

loves literary fiction, Nikes, and skateboarding, you read widely."

I laughed. Marcus was a remarkable young man, and if he kept up his reading pace, he'd out-read me in just a few years. "What did you find to recommend for the skateboarding obsession?"

"Tony Hawk's books of course." Josie laughed.

For the rest of the afternoon, my friend and I sat and recommended books, answered questions about Green's talk, and handed out literature about hospice. Between the two of us, we had personally recommended almost every book in my small Death and Dying section. Apparently, our guests today and presumably tonight were committed to thinking about death complexly and deeply, so I was thrilled to be able to suggest *Let's Take the Long Way Home*, a memoir about death and friendship to a woman whose best friend was just diagnosed with terminal breast cancer. Josie suggested *Stiff* by Mary Roach to the older man who was contemplating the options for his corpse. By the time four p.m. rolled around, the Death and Dying shelf was almost bare, and Josie and I were spent.

I gave her another hug, apologized for keeping her son at the store for another long day, and scooted my way out to Mart's waiting car with a wave to my staff. Their enthusiastic shouts of "good luck" and "*don't* break a leg" carried me safely to the car.

I HAVE ALWAYS WANTED someone to nominate me for one of those makeover shows. Back in the day, I hoped Clinton and Stacy would show up one day and whisk me away to New York, but now I was confident that I could impress Antoni from *Queer Eye* with my cooking skills. Tonight, though, Mart was basically all of the Fab Five thrown into one witty, kind best friend.

First, she fed me figs with goat cheese and honey while also refilling my wine glass just enough times that I was feeling relaxed but not loopy. Then, she washed my hair without soap using something called "the curly girl method" that involved the most luxurious conditioner, a towel that reminded me of the fancy shammies they used at car washes, and a spritz of coconut oil. My curls had never looked so good, especially when I slipped my sparkly headband back on and reined in a couple of the most unruly pieces until my hair looked perfectly like me and perfectly styled, too. I was clearly going to have to ask her to do my hair every day.

But she wasn't done. She painted my fingernails and worked some magic on my toes that made them look like I didn't stand (or scoot) on them all day. She even managed to coordinate the polish with Ollie's painting on my cast.

She didn't stop there, though. Next, she pulled out a long, flowing black skirt that I'd picked up years ago in a market in Morocco. That story has always sounded more elegant than it was. Really, I just only had five dollars to spend and this skirt fit my budget. I rarely wore it, though, because it was, well, it was a lot – like goth-girl meets Boho chic – a lot. But tonight, Mart paired it with a cut velvet blazer that my mom had bought me back in my days of fundraising so I'd have something to wear to a winter event. That and a simple camisole, my favorite rings, Mart's mom's jewelry, and my grandmother's bangles that, from a distance seemed to match my headband, and I was done.

I looked in the mirror and smiled. I looked good and, still, like me, not like me trying to put on a show. I spun around and smiled at Mart. "Thank you."

"You're most welcome." She took my shoulders and steered me toward the door. "All that primping has taken our available time. I will be there in twenty minutes, but your ride has already arrived."

I scooted down the hall and there was Daniel, in his one

suit but with a brand-new tie and, "Is that a pocket square?" I asked. "Tan would be so proud."

He lifted his jacket. "Maybe not because I didn't do a French tuck." He winked at me, and I cracked up.

"You may have watched a couple too many episodes of *Queer Eye* with me, big guy." I leaned up and kissed his cheek.

"Maybe," he said. "You look amazing."

I blushed. "Well, Mart does good work."

"Of course, but you are the art, my dear." He kissed me deeply and then tugged me toward the door.

I waved to Mayhem and Taco, who were already unconscious by the fire, and I blew a kiss to Aslan, who made it a point to not even open an eye in response. "I see we'll be sorely missed," I said.

"Terribly. I hope they make it," Daniel added.

I laughed and took his arm as he pulled me along to the truck.

THE RECEPTION WAS JUST BEGINNING when we arrived, and I found myself once again profoundly grateful for Mom and Dad's leadership of this part of the evening. Symeon was on hand overseeing the staff, and I gave him a wave as I came into the room. Henri and Bear were already mingling with the first guests, and I scooted over to give them quick hugs before I took up my station beside the donations table. Mom had arranged to have a comfortable chair on a small platform there for me so I could sit but still talk with folks from behind the table, and I was immensely grateful. My leg was throbbing, and I didn't know that I'd be able to stand on one foot the whole night.

Daniel stood near me and greeted everyone, taking it upon himself to explain my injury so that people didn't think me rude or lazy for sitting while they asked questions. He was definitely a keeper.

We had a steady stream of guests, and people were ever so generous with their donations – both in the large glass bowl that Mom had set up and seeded with bills and in the drop box for checks that she'd also arranged on a small table nearby so that people could leave checks without their information being visible.

During a lull in the traffic, Daniel leaned over and said, "We're getting pretty good at this raising money thing." I laughed, remembering the time recently when we'd blown the socks off both Mart and the organization she was supporting with her event.

"We are. Maybe we should go into business." I gave him a sly smile.

"Well, you already have a business, and I only have this one suit. So maybe we just do this for fun." He kissed the top of my head.

I liked that plan. Fundraising had been a great career for me back before I came to St. Marin's, but I appreciated the low-key life of a bookstore owner now. Still, it was good for my heart to support organizations I cared about, and hospice was definitely one of those organizations. Before I'd met Daniel, I'd always worried that I might die alone. I still worried about that sometimes, but at least I knew hospice would take me in and be sure I was comfortable in my last days if no one else was there to do it.

My thoughts strayed toward Bixley and his "alleged" murders. I could never understand how another person could willingly steal the life of another person, but in one sense I got it. If he thought they were suffering, well, then in his sick brain, I could understand how he might have felt he was helping. But when he saw their families suffering, when he looked at the pain he caused, that should have stopped him. But it didn't. He kept going. It was despicable.

I forced my mind back to the situation at hand by looking

across the room to see who I recognized. Pickle and his wife Lois were talking with Henri and Bear. Woody and a young woman – probably his daughter – were talking with my parents and Cate and Lucas, and I caught a glimpse of Elle wandering through the room.

I was looking for Mart when I nearly made eye contact with Max, but fortunately, I saw him before he saw me. I was surprised to see him here, but it was good that he'd shown up, for himself and for his restaurant, too.

I looked up at the woman Daniel had been telling about the work that hospice does with family support and was surprised to see he was talking with Cynthia. She caught my eye and smiled. "Hi Harvey. This guy here knows his stuff."

I swallowed hard. She seemed to be in a good mood, so I wondered what that meant about her conversation with Tuck. Had she had the second conversation with Tuck?

"Hi Cynthia. It's nice to see you here. I expect you're familiar with hospice's work." I smiled and hoped it looked sincere. I didn't believe she was Bixley's murderer, but I was still ill at ease with what Tuck had told me about her and all the pieces that pointed her way.

"Oh, very. They do amazing work. I recommend hospice all the time to terminal patients." She leaned down toward me and smiled again. "Even the ones who will probably die in the hospital." She looked me in the eye and held my gaze.

"Oh, you do," I said, a small smile growing on my lips. "I bet that's part of the records at the hospital, isn't it?"

She stood up and spread her hands wide at her hips. "As a matter of fact it is. Sheriff Tucker and I were talking about that very thing this afternoon."

I stood and scooted around the table. "Oh, I'm so glad to hear that. Really, really glad. I didn't want it to be you. I really didn't." I held out my hands, hoping she'd forgive me for suspecting her.

She reached over and pulled me into a hug. "I am so glad to hear that, Harvey." She pulled back and held me at arm's length. "It's natural you thought of me. My flippant attitude. My defensiveness. I was just so exhausted from trying to stop Bixley that when he died, the relief was palpable. But when the suspicion came soon after, I was resentful. I wanted someone to see what I had been doing all this time."

I nodded. I could completely understand that.

"I didn't help," Javier joined our little group. "I'm sorry I accused you. Dad loved you, and I should have trusted him, even if I couldn't trust you."

Cynthia let out a long sigh. "Terminal illnesses wear us down. They make us look for people to blame. We want someone to be responsible. I get it." She put a hand on Javier's arm. "And in this case, someone was responsible. It just wasn't me."

"The sheriff told me." Javier wrung his hands together. "I'm glad it wasn't you, but it was still someone."

"It was," Cynthia said. "But the sheriff is working on that. He told me they have a new clue." She and Javier wandered off into the crowd with a smile.

I rolled back around the table and leaned against Daniel. "They'd make a cute couple," I said.

Daniel rolled his eyes. "You can't sleuth, so you're turning to matchmaking?"

I shrugged. "Maybe."

We continued to answer questions and accept donations for a while, and about halfway through the reception, I heard the din of voices rise as John Green walked in. He looked like the perfect author – jeans and a plaid blazer with Chuck Taylors. He graciously greeted everyone who came his way, and I marveled that this time, at least, one of my heroes hadn't been a disappointment.

I was just about to make my way over to say hello when a

flash of bright red caught my eye. I looked over, and there was Damien in his Santa outfit. He even had a big sack that looked to be filled with boxes. He looked downright jovial, but for a reason I couldn't quite pin down, I wasn't happy to see him here.

18

I watched Damien move across the room for a few moments as I tried to figure out what was bothering me. He swaggered. He flirted. He acted like he was the reason for the party, and I cringed. I hated show-offs. I really hated show-offs who didn't really have any reason to show off. And I really, really hated show-offs who got their attention on the backs of other people's suffering. I decided then and there that Damien would finish out this season as Santa but that I wouldn't be inviting him back again. He had seemed a nice enough guy, but clearly, a taste of fame had gone to his head.

I shook off the icky feeling his behavior gave me and made my way over to Mr. Green, who smiled, hugged me, and thanked me – thanked ME – for this opportunity. As if I didn't already love him enough. I told him we were so grateful and then let him greet his adoring fans or hide in the bathroom, which would have been my option if I were him, while I headed over to see Mart.

She and Symeon were spiffing up the food and wine tables, and I took the opportunity to get a plate and steal a sip of Mart's wine. I only had one hand, so I opted to use it for nourishment instead of wine-tasting. I felt confident in my choice when the bacon-cheddar mini quiche reached my lips. "That guy of yours . . . he is a keeper."

Mart looked at me and smiled, "The quiche is good, right?"

"So good." I waved and headed back toward my table, ready to sit again while I ate the four additional quiches I had shamelessly added next to the meatballs and two baby carrots, for roughage. Daniel was talking up a potential donor, so I shifted my chair slightly to give them the illusion of privacy and studied the room again while I ate.

It was a good crowd and growing all the time. The doors to the gym had just opened, so the lobby was starting to empty. But still, I figured we had a full house, which wasn't always the case with big fundraisers. Sometimes people bought tickets to support the cause but didn't come to the event. But for John Green, people did both.

I was just wiping the crumbs from the last quiche crust from my blazer when I heard a strange sound from behind me. At first, I thought there was a cat in the room . . . it sounded like a kitten's yowl. But then, the sound got more persistent and louder. And it said my name. I spun around in my chair, trying to locate the source, but the din of conversation was disrupting my ability to locate where the sound was coming from. I touched Daniel's arm and then my ear, and then I scooted off to the edge of the room in the direction I thought the voice was coming from.

The further from the crowd I got, the clearer the sound was. It was a woman's voice, and she was definitely saying my name . . . but what was she saying after that? It sounded like "Harvey, big pow" or "whale sound." I just couldn't quite make it out . . . I eventually followed the woman's voice until I came to a blue door next to the weight room off the gym lobby. I put my ear against the metal door and listened.

"Harvey, watch out!" she said just as someone knocked my scooter out from under me and dropped a towel over my head.

A FEW MOMENTS LATER, the towel fell away, and I saw I was now crammed, scooter and all, into a very small, very dark space with someone who had, apparently, eighty two elbows. I tried to push myself upright to get some breathing room, but I couldn't get leverage without causing myself excruciating pain. So I said, "I'm sorry. I can't stand up. My ankle is broken."

The woman let out a huff of a laugh. "I know, Harvey. One second." She shifted, and then I was sitting on the floor with my back against what felt like metal shelving. I still couldn't see a thing, and while I recognized the woman's voice, I couldn't place it. "Thanks," I said. "And I'm sorry. Clearly, we know each other, but—"

"It's Cynthia." I felt her wedge herself next to me on the floor. "Guess we know who killed Bixley now."

"We do?"

"Well, yeah. Clearly, it was Damien, your Santa. He's the one who threw me in here." Cynthia sounded both angry and perplexed. "Isn't that how you ended up in here, too?"

I thought about it, trying to capture any glimpse I might have had of Damien or his Santa suit, but I had nothing. "If he put you in here, then I expect he did the same to me. But I didn't see him." I put the towel, which I'd felt next to me, into her hands. "He put this over my head. I always keep my phone on me, but this one time, it's sitting on the table. Ugh."

Cynthia sighed. "Well, clearly, we need to get out of here and tell someone."

"Clearly. You tried the door, I'm sure."

I could almost feel her roll her eyes. "Clearly. It's locked and heavy. I tried slamming into a few times, but all I got was an achy shoulder."

I shuddered at the thought of me trying to slam open the door with my broken ankle. I'd just gotten over the blow to my head, and I didn't want another pain to carry around. "Right. So then, we need to make some noise. I heard you calling for me, which is why I came over."

"Okay, let's try that again." She raised her voice and started shouting help.

Between her shouts, I called out to Daniel, the person I knew who was closest to the door. We called for a couple of minutes, but no one came.

I took a deep breath, and that's when I noticed I couldn't hear any sound from outside the room. I pried myself off the floor and leaned over my scooter to put my ear against the door. I didn't hear voices at all. I strained my ears to listen, and then, I could make out a steady hum of a single tone. "Oh no, Green has started his talk, which means no one will be out in the lobby to hear us."

I sat down on my scooter and groaned.

"Okay, let's think. Someone will look for us, right? I was supposed to sit with Javier, so he'll probably be wondering."

I perked up. "Right, and John Green is one of my favorite authors, so Daniel will definitely be worried when he doesn't see me in inside." I let my head roll side to side while I thought. "So we just have to help them figure out where to look."

I heard Cynthia stand up beside me. "Alright, let's do this." I felt her slide something into my hand and realized it was a small, round piece of metal. "They must keep the extra weights here."

"Ah, I didn't recognize it because I do my best to avoid gyms and the like."

Cynthia laughed. "I bet you can keep a steady beat, though."

"Don't you know it. I was the secret girl drummer for New Kids on the Block back in the day. They didn't invite me on

their recent tour, though, so I'm through with them." I didn't
know why I was cracking jokes when my new friend and I had
been locked in a closet, but I appreciated Cynthia's laughter.

Then, we began to bang. Steadily and as loudly as we could.
We slammed our metal pucks against the shelving again and
again until after what seemed like thirty minutes, I heard a key
in the lock.

The light blinded me, but I'd know Daniel's silhouette
anywhere. "You found us," I said.

"I will find you," Daniel quoted in his best Daniel Day
Lewis voice, and then I felt him tug my scooter out of the way
and half guide, half-lift me to the door. "Now, help me find who
did this." He wasn't joking around anymore.

"It was Santa," I said.

IT WAS ONLY a matter of minutes before we had, via text
message, gotten all our friends out of the auditorium to help us
look for Damien. Well, all of our friends except for Henri and
Bear, who were on the stage with Green and whom we didn't
want to alarm, and Tuck, who was standing as a quasi-body-
guard near the stage. Green had made no request for such, but
all of us agreed that it was better to have a presence of protec-
tion than to send a world-famous author onto a stage in a high
school gym totally unguarded.

We did text Tuck, but he didn't respond, and I didn't think
we could wait until he either heard his text alert or checked his
phone, so we broke up into the group and spread out around
the school, hoping that Damien had kept on his Santa outfit
and would, thus, be easier to spot in the crowd. Mart, Symeon,
and Elle took the lobby and the exterior of the building. Pickle,
Mom and Dad searched the school hallways, and Woody, Cate,
Lucas, and I each took a quadrant of the gym bleachers while
Daniel searched beneath them.

A quick scan of the auditorium revealed that Damien had decided going on as St. Nick was a bit too obvious for whatever nefarious thing he was about to do. That meant we had to search row by row and face by face until we found him. I had chosen the set of bleachers nearest the platform and to Green's left, and I settled myself on the bench of my scooter just in the shadows beside the bleachers and began to look. I was on about the fifth row of faces when my phone buzzed in my pocket.

"Found Santa's suit. And these," Mart's text said. I zoomed in on the photo and broke into a cold sweat. It was a box for bullets. Damien was planning to shoot someone.

"Any sense of where he went?" I replied, knowing that a pile of red velour and empty cardboard wasn't much to go on.

"Your dad says these are rifle bullets."

Alarm raced through my body as I tried to text Woody, Daniel, Cate, and Lucas as quickly as I could: "Look up!! Look at the back of the room, too." I didn't have time to explain, but I figured with the distance a bullet from a rifle could go, Damien wouldn't be seated at close range.

I threw discretion to the wind and hauled myself up until I was standing on my scooter while I held onto the bleacher rails for support. My movement must have caught Tuck's eye because he stared at me, and I waved my phone. He pulled his from its case on his belt and then looked at me again, this time with alarm in his eyes. Then, he steadied himself and climbed the bleachers with speed but not panic.

A second later, John Green was hunched behind the podium, and Tuck was shooing Henri and Bear off the platform. I was checking to be sure Green was safe when my phone buzzed again. Woody this time: "Catwalk above far basketball goal."

I spun my head to the left and saw him, crouched with a rifle on the railing. "Get down!" I screamed as loudly as I could, and near me, everyone did . . . then, I heard the cry spread around the room, and like a horrific version of the wave, everyone in the room crouched low, trying to take cover behind wooden bleachers that were only a few inches high.

The sound of hundreds of people moving around was quite loud, but Damien's voice cut through it all. "I'm not going to hurt any of you," he said.

I peeked out from where I was now trying to squat one-legged on my rolling scooter and saw Damien with a bullhorn to his mouth. "I'm just here to take care of one bit of business, and then all of you can go back to your reading."

"Sheriff Mason, please step out." Damien's voice was smooth and even. " It's you I would like to speak with."

I tried to send Tuck telepathic messages to stay down, don't walk out, but even before I thought those words, he was stepping out, raising his hand, dropping his weapon behind him.

My heart stopped, I'm fairly sure, as I watched my friend walk out and face the man with the rifle. I had known he would do that, that if his making himself completely vulnerable meant that he might save someone else's life, then there was going to be no question that he was walking out. And still, I'd hoped he'd make another choice.

"You are responsible," Damien said as his voice echoed through the now nearly silent gymnasium. "Because you didn't catch him, I had to take action."

I gasped, and then, like checkers falling into place in a Connect Four game, I realized what I had already known subconsciously: Damien had killed Bixley. The syringe by the sleigh. The bag of syringes in the back room. Even the pride Damien took in drawing so much attention for being the Santa Bixley died on. It was all because he had injected Bixley himself . . . and because he was proud of it.

"You mean because I couldn't catch Bixley before he killed someone else?" Tuck's voice was steady and clear, but I could see his hands shaking just slightly as he held them in the air. I swept my eyes from Tuck toward Damien, but they snagged on Lu, there in the front row, pinned down as she watched her husband face off, unarmed, against a man who wanted to shoot him. It was the look on her face that did it, that popped open the question that had been haunting me since Woody found the syringe.

Without thinking, I rolled out into the floor and turned toward Damien, who immediately trained his rifle on me. Only then, did I realize that, once again, my curiosity had put me in danger. Somewhere further toward the back of the room, I heard Daniel hiss, "Harvey, no!" But it was too late. I'd leaped in, and now, I might as well follow through.

"But Bixley was already slurring and stumbling when he came to the store? If you killed him, why was that?"

Damien's face broke into a grin that reminded me, in the most terrifying way, of Jack Nicholson's character in *The Shining*. "Oh, that's easy. He wasn't just a murderer. He was also a drunk. Probably helped him sleep at night." Damien sighed. "He kind of helped me out there, made it easier to hide the symptoms of the insulin overdose until it was too late."

I nodded, not sure what to do now that I had my answer, but my brain had registered that Damien had just confessed. And unless he was the world's most absent-minded murderer, that confession meant he didn't think he was going to get out of here alive. I felt my heart sink. It wasn't even a school day, and yet, we were going to have another mass shooting in a school.

I scanned the crowd quickly and tried to keep my eyes moving as I saw both Woody and my dad climbing the ladders to the catwalk where Damien perched. Why the oldest men available were doing this, I didn't know. It felt like maybe Lucas or Daniel should have been the ones to attempt to wrestle a gun out of someone's hands, but I wasn't about to suggest a change of tactic right now. Although, I wasn't thrilled anyone was going up there, let alone my dad.

A quick glimpse at Tuck's face told me he wasn't happy either, but since he couldn't stop them, he drew Damien's focus back to him. "What did you want me to do, Damien?"

"I wanted you to catch him before he killed my dad." Damien's voice broke as he spoke, and I felt just the tiniest bit of sympathy as I remembered him telling me about his father, about how he'd died before meeting his granddaughter. Now, to know that he died because Bixley killed him, I could begin to understand Damien's anger. Not his actions, but his anger – that I could sort of get.

"Damien, you have every right to be angry. You can even be angry at me, but please, let's not take this out on anyone here." Tuck's voice was firm but there was an edge of pleading to it. "Please."

"No one needs to worry, Sheriff, as long as I get what I want," Damien said, the megaphone in one hand and the rifle still trained on Tuck in the other.

I said a silent prayer that Tuck could keep him talking because I'd just seen that Daniel, Elle, Mart, Symeon, Lucas, and Cate had silently opened the doors at the back of the gym and were gesturing to the guests to leave. Slowly but surely – and so quietly I didn't think I'd ever excuse the usual stomping on bleachers again, if I survived that was – the bleachers were emptying. I didn't know what Damien would do when he began to see people leaving, but I hoped that Tuck – with my help – could keep his eye trained on the front of the room.

"What do you want, Damien?" I said, hoping that if I could keep Damien looking from me to Tuck at least more people would get out.

"I want him to issue a public apology, and then I want him to resign." Damien's voice was firm and clear, and I almost breathed a sigh a relief. Tuck could totally do that and then take his job back tomorrow. But then Damien continued, "And I want him to feel what my dad felt."

I grimaced. I had been hoping this was some kind of stunt, that the rifle was more for showmanship than action, but apparently, that wasn't the case. "You don't have to do this, Damien," I said.

"Oh, I know I don't have to," Damien said as he swung his megaphone and his rifle barrel back toward me. "I want to."

A cold sweat broke out on my body, and I wheeled closer to Tuck. I don't know why. But I did it. "Damien, please. Come down. We can all talk."

Out of the corner of my eye, I saw Tuck give a slight nod, and I took that to mean he liked that I was keeping Damien talking. "Everyone else can go. We can just sit and talk. I'll even record Tuck apologizing and resigning, load it to the store's Instagram page. You know we're getting a lot of traffic tonight because of this event." For a split second, I thought about John Green, crouched behind a podium, and felt immensely sorry that his kindness had left him in this situation. "Everyone will know what happened, Damien. Please." I could hear the begging in my voice, and I hoped Damien could, too. I wasn't ready to believe he was beyond hope, not yet.

For a second, his megaphone drooped, and I thought maybe we had a break, but then he raised it back up. "I like the idea of recording, Harvey. But I want you to record everything, including what I'm about to do to your sheriff friend there."

I gasped. He wanted me to livestream him murdering Tuck. I could not do that. I just could not. I spun my head toward Tuck, and he held my gaze as he said, "It's okay, Harvey. Do as he says."

"No, Tuck, I can't do that. I won't."

"Yes, you will, Harvey. You will." Tuck's eyes felt like they were boring holes into mind, and for some reason, I thought I saw something more, a message that I couldn't quite get but that was saying it would be okay.

"I'm coming down, but if anyone tries anything, I will shoot up this room, and we'll have an even more terrible Christmas story to tell in St. Marin's." This time, I didn't have any doubt he meant what he said.

So we all sat still, the fifty or so people still in the bleachers, Tuck, John Green behind the podium, Henri, Bear, and I as Damien climbed down the ladder past Woody, who had made it to the top just as Damien issued his ultimatum, and across the floor to us.

"Take a seat, Sheriff. Let's be sure that Harvey gets your whole face in the picture. Don't want none of those half-face videos that people post, now do we?" Damien seemed jovial now, like he was returning to his proud self as a social media celebrity.

Tuck gave me another meaningful stare as he lowered himself to the stage and then looked at Lu, who looked terrified but resolute. She trusted her husband, and she wasn't going to leave him either.

I took out my phone, opened Instagram stories, and pressed video. Then, I showed Damien the screen so he could see I was recording. I trained the camera on Tuck, and he began.

It felt like I was watching one of those TV dramas where the terrorists makes someone record a confession. It felt like that because it was just like that. Tuck said his name. He said he was guilty of not having stopped Bixley from committing murder. He said he was resigning because St. Marin's deserved a better sheriff, and then he handed Damien his badge. It was heartbreaking. I tried not to cry behind the camera.

"Very good, Sheriff. That's perfect," Damien said before looking over at me. "Now, Harvey, don't stop filming."

I stared at him over my phone and gasped when he pulled an insulin syringe out of his back pocket. I'd seen enough of those things to recognize it instantly, and the terror climbed my spine like a spider. Tuck slid back, away from Damien, but Damien raised the gun level with Tuck's face, and the sheriff froze.

"I'd say I'm sorry, Sheriff, but I'm really not. I'm sorry my dad died before you could stop this guy. I'm sorry I had to do your job and stop him. But I'm not sorry for making you pay for that. Not at all."

Tuck stared at the gun and then the syringe. I could see, from the corner of my eye, Daniel and Lucas making their way silently to the front of the gym. I was praying they'd make it before that syringe reached Tuck's arm, but Damien was closing in on the sheriff. A few more seconds and that needle would be killing Tuck.

And even though Bear was there, could maybe save his friend, I knew Damien would never let that happen.

Daniel was just a few feet away when Damien uncapped the syringe and grabbed Tuck's arm, shifting the rifle into his side as he did.

Then, a shot rang out.

19

When I got up from having my face land squarely on the floor of the gym, I expected to see at least one of the people I loved mortally wounded, but instead, there, on the ground writhing, was Damien. His shin was bleeding, and he looked as confused as I was.

I quickly glanced around and saw Bear lay Tuck's pistol on the podium before he reached down and gave John Green his hand. Green, for his part, looked appropriately frazzled but also grateful. Henri led him out of the gym as Tuck picked up first Damien's rifle and then the syringe from where it had fallen by the wheel of my scooter. Then, Bear moved in, tore the sleeve off his dress shirt, and bandaged Damien's wound. Once that was done, Tuck cuffed him and then looked at me and said, "May we?"

I gave him a puzzled look, but when he looked at my scooter I understood. "Sure. I'll just wait here."

Tuck nodded and then sat Damien on the scooter and rolled him across the gym. Then, and only then, did I start to shake.

. . .

A COUPLE OF HOURS LATER, everyone gathered at our house to debrief and drink lots of calming tea. I was glad I'd picked up a fresh batch of chamomile from my favorite tea shop in Annapolis a couple weeks back.

John Green had gone back to his hotel by Uber since he didn't want to ask Daniel to drive him and maybe because he was – justifiably – a little terrified to be around any of us. But he had only left after staying, still, to sign the books of the few dozen people who hung around to ask him. Those people, I figured, were either such hard-core fans that they simply could not pass up an opportunity to meet their favorite author *or* complete psychopaths. Either way, Green was gracious, and I knew his place in my top tier of author admiration would never waver.

"Harvey, is there any way to get that video down?" Elle asked as she handed me a cup of tea and a ginger cookie.

I took a big bite of the soft, scrumptious cookie, and then I smiled. "I actually didn't record anything."

Every head in the room whipped toward me. "What did you say, Harvey?" Lu asked as she leaned in. Tuck hadn't made it over yet, but he'd insisted Lu come be with us instead of waiting alone at home or at the station. I was really glad she was there.

"I didn't record it," I said again. "I just hit the photo button, and Damien believed I was recording." I looked around the room. "I guess you all did, too."

Lu sat back in her chair, and I saw her shoulders start to shake. Mart slid in next to her and let her cry.

"That's pretty incredible for a dude who fancied himself God's gift to Instagram," Cate said. "Studly Santa can't tell if a video is recording or not. Go figure."

I smiled at the idea that my nickname for Damien had stuck, but then I pictured his face as he moved toward Tuck. Felt like maybe Satan Santa was better somehow.

"Thank goodness," Lucas added. "I hope people would have been understanding, but given the way people blow up over everything on social media, I think it might have taken Tuck some time to recover from that one."

"Yes, thank you, Harvey," Lu said. "You did just the right thing, even under all that pressure. I couldn't even move . . ." Her voice trailed off. I couldn't imagine what it must have felt like to see her husband almost die. I didn't even want to imagine it.

"Let's face it. I could have as easily not recorded it by accident. I know at least a few of you have gotten a 'butt photo' from me when I sat on my phone and accidentally texted the image. I'm not the most tech savvy." I was feeling awkward with the focus on me for just *not* doing something. Bear had actually stopped Damien.

Now, though, the real hero had dozed off on his wife's shoulder. Bear looked peaceful. I knew that many people – me included – find sleep a natural response to a really stressful situation. If Bear himself were speaking, he'd probably tell us about the fall after an adrenal response – at least that's what he'd said when I'd conked out after I'd been in danger a few months back. His body was giving him space, time to process what had happened.

Henri put her hand on Bear's cheek and smiled at me. "Something tells me you may know exactly why Damien did this. Am I right?"

I sighed. "I think I know. Maybe." I told them everything Damien had said about his father, about the way Bixley had killed him just before his dad got to meet Damien's niece. The room grew very quiet and very heavy.

"How long ago was that?" Woody asked.

"That I'm not sure of," I said. "I didn't ask a lot of questions when Damien was telling me the story because I didn't realize, at the time, it was a clue, you know?"

Woody nodded. "I was just reading *The Beautiful Mystery*, and Gamache and Beauvoir talk about how an event often sets off a murder."

"Clearly, I need to read that book," Daniel said. "Seems like we have enough murder here that it might be worth it to know more."

I squeezed his hand. "Well, that's a novel, but I do think Louise Penny makes a compelling psychology of murder in her books."

"If that's the case, then something set Damien off last week," Cate said as she stretched. "I wonder what it was."

Just then, the front door opened, and Tuck came in. He looked haggard, not that I'd tell him that. That word is never taken as a compliment. Mart hopped up and got him a mug of tea as Elle slid onto the floor to allow Tuck to sit next to his wife. "You're done for the night?" Lu asked.

Tuck nodded. "He confessed, obviously. Not much choice there."

"It was about his dad's murder," Symeon said.

"It was." Tuck sighed, "And finally, I don't have to say 'alleged' murder. Damien had actually found proof that Bixley was killing people."

Everyone in the room sat up a little straighter as Dad said, "He did?!"

"Yep, apparently, Danita had videotaped Bixley committing the murder of Petra's father."

I gasped. "What?! Why didn't she turn over the video?"

"That's a good question. My only guess," Tuck ran his hands down his face, "is that she was scared. She told Damien though."

Stephen groaned. "And when she wouldn't give you the tape, Damien killed her."

"Yes."

I leaned my head back against the chair and let the heaviness of all that sink into me. One man killing two people because another man killed many. I wondered if Damien would ever realize the irony of his actions. I doubted it. It seemed to me if you were sick enough to revel in celebrity caused by a murder you committed because your own father was murdered, self-awareness probably wasn't a high priority.

Tiffany suddenly leaned forward. "Did you tell Cynthia and Javier?" Her voice was tight but hopeful.

"First two phone calls I made," the sheriff said. "I'll give them the whole story tomorrow." Then he stood and helped Lu to her feet. "Now, though, I'm going home to sleep." He looked over at Bear. "Unlike our friend here, I would not be able to walk if I slept like that."

"Oh, he will need an adjustment first thing in the morning," Henri said as she gave Bear a nudge and watched him stir. "I'll fill you in tomorrow, Mister. Let's get you home."

Bear stretched and sighed. "Sorry, everyone. Adrenal—"

"We know," several of us said at the same time.

"Go home and get some rest – all of you." I looked around the room at my friends. "I'll see you around town tomorrow."

I scooted toward the door and distributed hats and scarves as each person headed out. Soon, only Tuck and Lu hung back, and when I looked at the sheriff, I knew he'd done so on purpose.

"What is it, Tuck?"

"I just wanted to say thank you, Harvey. Your quick thinking with that camera saved me." The sheriff leaned over and gave me a firm hug.

I smiled. "Do me a favor in return and satisfy my curiosity."

Tuck rolled his eyes but didn't walk out.

"Bixley was obviously drunk when he came to the store that night. But why did he come? I mean when you're tipsy, a bookstore isn't most people's first choice. "

"Ah, yes, Damien did clear that up. He'd invited Bixley on

the pretext that he wanted to thank the 'hero-nurse' for his good care of his father. Told him he had a special gift for him that could only be delivered when he was in costume." The sheriff shook his head.

"And Bixley fell for that? Why would it matter that Damien was playing Santa?" Daniel looked as puzzled as I felt.

"I asked the same thing," Tuck said as he slid a knit cap over his shaved head. "Apparently, Damien promised Bixley that he'd arranged a press conference where Santa would be thanking medical workers for their fine service."

"Ah, so Bixley's hero complex was revved up. He was celebrating, hence the drinks," I said.

"What an egotistical jack—" Lu spat.

"Precisely, but Damien knew just what buttons to push. The man is no idiot."

I sighed. Clearly not, but he was sick – sick enough to kill two people.

I closed the door on our friends and turned back to face Mart and Daniel. "I'm not sure I can sleep yet. Feel like watching something?"

"As long as it's not *Murder, She Wrote*," Mart said.

"Agreed," I said as I slid back into my chair. "Agreed."

20

The next couple of weeks whizzed by. The store was busier than ever – fed by good word of mouth, a dedicated Instagram effort by our favorite fan, Galen, and the remnants of scandal from Bixley's death and Damien's arrest. Apparently, he'd met someone through his social media posts, and she was continuing in his stead with posts about his heroism and bravery. Neither Damien nor his devotee ever denied that he'd murdered Bixley and Danita. In fact, they bragged about it so openly that Damien said there was talk about him not having to stand trial, a rumor Tuck quashed quickly by pointing out that the law requires due process and a fair trial to every citizen, even stupid ones. The trial wouldn't happen until the new year, but none of us had any doubt that Damien would be held accountable for his crimes.

I tried to put the whole mess behind me as best I could, and given the swift sales and the follow-up to Green's event – through which we raised over forty thousand for our local hospice – I was busy enough not to lose myself in the gossip. Mom had decided she was going to make goal of doing a major charity function every two months, and she wanted the store to participate by selling books related to each organization's work. We were still making our schedule, but I was enjoying the thought of dedicating part of the store's earnings and my time to this new mission of mom's.

Plus, it was the holidays, and between the Hallmark movies that Mart and I were binging on and the escapades that they were inspiring for her, Symeon, Daniel, and me – let's just say ice skating with a scooter is not wise – I was staying busy in my off hours, too. It was a good few weeks, but of course, something always happens.

On Christmas Eve morning, we opened the store as usual, and soon after, Max Davis strolled in with a wheelchair. I looked behind him to see if maybe an aging parent was making his way on a walker and would switch to the chair once in the store, but it appeared Max was alone. Alone and coming right for me. I sighed. I could not imagine what this was about, but I knew I wasn't going to like it.

"Happy Holidays, Max," I said with as much gusto as I could.

"Merry Christmas," he said pointedly as if lobbing back my kind greeting with the weapon of a holiday phrase. "I brought you a gift." He thrust the wheelchair in my direction.

I stared. "You brought me a wheelchair?" I looked over at my scooter and back at the wheelchair. "Why?"

"You aren't exactly graceful on that, er, thing," he said. "In this, you can be cared for until you heal."

I felt my blood pressure rise and gritted my teeth. "I don't want to be 'cared for' that way, Max. I do just fine with my scooter." I should have stopped talking then, but I couldn't help myself. "Who, exactly, do you think is going to push me around in this thing anyway? Or will I be wheeling myself around?" I thought of my friends in wheelchairs who were masterful at moving through tight spaces and around corners. If Max thought I wasn't graceful on my scooter, he hadn't seen anything yet.

"Are you ashamed of needing help?" Max's eyebrows were almost up at his hairline. "I didn't take you as someone who is too prideful to accept assistance, Harvey."

I clenched my fists and took a deep breath. "There is no shame in being in a wheelchair if it is truly helpful or necessary, Max. If I needed one – which I don't – I would use it. But I will not make more of my injury than it is, even if that means I look ungraceful." I grabbed my scooter and pushed past him to the front door. "Now, I would like you to go."

Max huffed and began wheeling the chair to the door.

"No, leave the chair," I said firmly.

"But, you just said--"

"I don't need it, but hospice always needs more chairs for their clients."

Max turned a shade of red that fit the season and walked past me, mumbling something about people being ungrateful under his breath.

"Oh, I'm grateful, Max. I'll even give the chair in your honor. Thank you," I said with false joviality just as the door closed behind him.

That man.

Fortunately, the man I had actually chosen, the one who didn't belittle me or tell me I didn't know what I needed, had a much better gift. On Christmas morning, I opened a small box to find a folded sheet of paper. When I opened it, there was a picture of a Neapolitan Mastiff puppy. "Coming home in three weeks" the note said.

I looked from the wrinkled, charcoal gray face to Daniel and back again. "What is this?"

He took the paper from me and said, "That, Harvey, is a puppy. His name is Steamroller. Merry Christmas."

"You got me a dog for Christmas?" I asked as the gift sank in. "A one-hundred-twenty-five-pound dog?

"Well, he'll only weigh about five pounds when we pick him and Dozer up."

"Dozer?" I was lost with all the equipment names.

"His brother, my new dog." Daniel's grin was huge. He was over the moon about these two new pups.

I looked over at Mayhem and Taco snoozing by the fire by the Christmas tree and then glanced at Mart's gifts stacked nearby for her to open when she returned from visiting her family. "You do realize that this means we'll have four dogs between us, don't you?"

Just then, Aslan mewled from her spot beside me. I scratched her jaw and said, "I know, girl. But we'll teach them who is queen."

"Yes, we will," Daniel said as he kissed my cheek. "I just figured we'd get a house with a big yard and the largest doggy door out there."

"A house, huh?" I smiled. My life was good, so good. I just hoped the internet could give me tips on how to remove drool stains.

SCRIPTED TO SLAY

A FREE PREVIEW OF BOOK 6 IN THE ST. MARIN'S COZY
MYSTERY SERIES

I sat in my reading chair and looked out the window. The snow had started overnight, and the forecast was for it to continue well into the morning. I was so excited. We almost never got snow out here on Maryland's Eastern Shore, and I loved snow, especially if it snowed me in, which was the case today. All of St. Marin's was basically shut down because, well, because we didn't have a snowplow. The town had never invested in one, and I had to say that seemed wise to me. Now, all of us could just stay in and read with hot cocoa and extra marshmallows.

Many of my neighbors were not of my perspective, though, my mother included. She had texted no fewer than nine times to lament how awful it was that she couldn't get out. After the ninth message, I had replied, "Urgent meeting today? Medications to fill? Friend without food?" Her extended silence followed by the acidic "Hardy har har" in reply told me that she'd gotten my point. My mother was retired, and while she stayed busy with charity events - a volunteer gig that she was incredibly good at - she had no need to go out. She and Dad had enough food to keep the town fed in light of the apocalypse, and they'd put in a whole house generator when they'd bought their condo. So even if the power went out, they'd be warm and toasty.

As would I by my fire with a lap blanket, my chubby cat Aslan, and my hound dog Mayhem. Plus, I wouldn't have that pesky hum of the generator. My bookstore was closed for the day, and I was going to enjoy the quiet. Alone. It was blissful.

My best friend and roommate Mart had stayed over at her boyfriend Symeon's house the night before, and my fiancé Daniel was out and about with his tow truck helping those brave souls who thought they could drive in snow but couldn't or who had to drive because of work out of ditches. He'd be gone all day most likely, so I was already hunkering down with Angie Thomas's new book *Concrete Rose* and coffee. I could pretend I'd miss Daniel - and I would in a mild kind of way that gave me a little pause when I thought too hard about it - but mostly I was just giddy with the quiet. The quiet of snow was absolute, and it felt like my spirit needed that relief.

I HAD JUST MADE it through the first half of Thomas's stellar book when my phone dinged. I rolled my eyes, expecting Mom to be whining about how she can't stand to be trapped in her luxury condo on the water for one more minute, and picked up my phone. It was Daniel. "Headed down the shore to help with a multi-car pile-up near the Bay Bridge. Don't think I'll make it back safely tonight. I'm sorry. Stay warm."

I sighed, let myself ponder the lack of "I love you" in his message for a minute, and then remembered that he was out helping people. . . and that this meant I had the entire day to do with as I wished. "Oh, I"m sure everyone will be so grateful. Drive safely," I replied in kind with a pang of something I wasn't willing to consider. Then I tucked the phone under my leg and started reading again.

Sometime around 3pm and 18 slices of cheese and a bowl of popcorn later, I unfolded myself from under Aslan, much to her annoyance, and decided to don all the cold weather clothing I owned - scarf, hat with ear flaps, a massive eggplant-purple parka, and my fleece-lined boots to go for a walk. Mayhem would have gladly done her business at the edge of the porch to avoid getting her feet wet, but given the opportunity to pull me bodily through snow banks, she managed to muster up a tail wag as I put on her leash.

Once we were out the door, the bracing cold and the bright light of the newly-showing sun told me we'd made the right call. I could feel the blood starting to pick up in my circulatory system just to keep my body warm. So Mayhem and I headed out through the six or so inches of show that my friends in the northern climes would scoff out as "a dusting." Here, though, this was a named Blizzard, Blizzard Paco. I didn't understand this phenomenon of naming every storm, not just hurricanes, but at least I knew how to address the air around me as I walked. "Paco, thanks for this. I appreciate the day off and the beauty. So yeah, thanks," I said out loud as Mayhem and I turned onto the wonderland that was our town's Main Street after a snow storm.

Everything was glittering, and there were tufts of snow on the streetlamps and awnings. A road crew had managed to do one pass up the street, so the piles of snow by the sidewalk were substantial. Up ahead, I could see some of my fellow shop-keepers beginning to shovel their square feet of sidewalk. I sighed and decided to do my duty, too, even though I kind of wanted to simply go on back home, finish Thomas's book, and binge the new season of Glow Up that I'd been saving for a special day.

I trudged over to the hardware store and bought their only

snow shovel. It was a massive thing, bright yellow and built like a front-end loader, but it did the trick. Within a few minutes, I had the sidewalk in front of my store clear, and I was making my way across the parking lot between my shop and the garden center. Mayhem had insisted on going into the bookstore, so she was now watching me intently from the warmth of my shop's front window. She had such a hard life.

I was just heading back to stow my new shovel at my shop after digging out a couple more store fronts for friends when I heard my name. I looked up from where'd I'd been trying to pry individual snow flakes from the concrete and saw Max Davies, the man who owned the French restaurant up the street from me, smiling and waving. Well, I think it was what you'd call a wave. Max's hand moved like it was a mechanized part of an early robot, all stiff and awkward. But he was definitely calling me, and soon his stiff waved turned into an awkward beckoning motion.

I shot Mayhem a look and secretly hoped she'd nudge the store door open and make a break for it so I could chase her down in the snow rather than talk to Max, but she just looked back at me, forehead wrinkled, like she was enjoying the strange show. I sighed, propped my shovel against my store door, and walked down to Max.

Max Davies was a nice enough man if you liked arrogant, know-it-alls who think they are God's gift to, well, you in particular. Max had a serious thing for me, and while I always felt awkward saying that when someone asked why he kissed my hand for so long on every greeting, it was the truth, a truth I hated. He'd been pursuing me in his really off-base way ever since I'd moved to town more than a year ago, and despite the fact that Daniel and I were engaged, he hadn't slowed down in his pursuits at all. More than once I'd thought about telling him what he could do with his slobbering hand kisses, but St. Marin's is a small town. . . and I didn't want drama. . . okay, I didn't want conflict. Drama just seemed to be part of Max's way in the world.

Now, he was grinning at me like he'd just seen snow for the first time, and I braced myself. This couldn't be good. "Hi Max. What's up?" I said as I stopped a safe two feet away and kept my hands in my pockets.

"Bonjour, Mademoiselle," he said with his fake French accent. Max was from Baltimore, and while he made the best risotto I'd ever had, there was nothing actually French about him. "I see you have been working hard for hours, and I wanted to invite you in for your favorite to help warm you up."

I looked at my watch. I'd been shoveling for 30 minutes, not exactly hours, but I was cold . . . and if he was talking about his mushroom risotto, he was right. It was my favorite, and I was starving. Still, I hesitated.

The problem was that Max often thought I should like things even when I didn't. One time, he'd brought me a chocolate dessert flavored with orange liqueur after I'd told him specifically that I didn't like chocolate and fruit together. He had made some comment about me just needing help to train my palate, and I had shoved the dessert in front of Mart, who had devoured it with revenge-filled glee. So while I was tempted by the idea of risotto, I couldn't be sure he'd actually give me risotto. Plus, I could be sure he would be there, and that alone was just about enough reason to walk away.

But I was cold and hungry, and a quick scan of the street told me that no one was going to come, not even my dog, to rescue me. So I nodded and trudged along behind him into his restaurant. It was warm inside, and Max had a fire roaring in the fireplace that was the centerpiece of the room. I could hear someone knocking around in the kitchen. For a moment, I wondered if it was Symeon, Mart's boyfriend, but then I remembered that her text earlier had said he'd taken the day and that Max was okay with it because the sous chef was available for the limited fare they'd offer to anyone who stopped by. Anyone being me, it seemed. The rest of the dining room was empty.

Max gestured for me to sit in the front window, and I wondered if he wanted to use me as bait for other customers. But then I realized, with a little surprise, that it was actually the best seat in the house. The raised platform by the window gave me a view up and down Main Street, and I could see the white lights that most shopkeepers left up in their windows year round reflecting off the snow as dusk began to settle in. The sky was that pearl-gray of a winter's afternoon, and with the slight breeze off the water that was picking up tendrils of snow, it looked like a postcard. I found myself strangely grateful that Max had invited me in.

Even when he showed up with a warm mug of wine without asking me if I'd like any, I couldn't muster up enough snark to comment. Instead, I took the heavy ceramic mug in both hands and took a sip of the sweet white wine that was spicy and lemony, and then I sighed. It was really good. Max then brought me a salad full of spicy arugula and dressed with a vinagarette that was tangy and rich. Finally, he carried over a beautiful, ceramic bowl full of his mushroom risotto, and I almost groaned out loud. I don't know what he did to make that dish so amazing, but on this evening in this setting, it felt like I was going to be eating ambrosia, the food of the gods.

After Max set down the bowl, I thought he might decide to join me, especially given the quiet in his restaurant, but instead, he smiled and walked away. I was grateful. There was something about this meal in this place by myself that felt sacred, special, and while I knew that I should be missing Daniel, I also knew that some of the most memorable times in my life were when I had chosen to be alone. I had a feeling this would be one of those times.

I savored every morsel of that risotto and had just set down my spoon when Max returned with a slice of apple gallette that looked divine. It was caramelized on the bottom, and across the top, Max had drizzled just the lightest bit of cinnamon glaze. As he set the plate in front of me, he said, "I decided ice cream might be too much, but if you'd like some--"

I put up my hand. "No, this is perfect." I looked up at my host and smiled, maybe really smiled at him for the first time. "Thank you, Max. This has been an incredible meal." And I meant it. Somehow, this was exactly what I needed to end this restful, magical day.

I ate my dessert and waited for Max to return so I could ask for my bill. When he came back, he handed me a waiter's notebook, and inside it said, "For Harvey. With my compliments. Thank you for treasuring my food as I treasure you." I stared at the note and smiled. Then I looked up and waved to Max who was standing at the bar with a small smile on his face.

I never would have guessed it, but tonight Max had shown that some woman, some day would win a fine man's heart. I smiled and bowed my head. Then, I slipped on my coat and hat and headed toward the door.

The sun was almost down, and I took one last deep breath of the warm air before I stepped back into the cold again. Then, I heard Max yell, "Get help, Harvey. Get help!"

Bless my heart, I almost didn't turn around because I assumed this was some ruse on Max's part to get me back in so he could ruin a lovely evening with skeeziness. But something about his tone of voice sounded authentic, so I stepped back inside and looked around. He was nowhere to be seen. "Max?"

"Over here, Harvey. Call 911." His voice was coming from behind the bar.

As I rushed over, I took out my phone and dialed, but as soon as the operator picked up, I realized I didn't know what to tell her. So I jumped up and stretched over the bar so I could see. There, crumpled in a heap, was a young woman. "Is she alive, Max?"

He stared up at me and gave a little shake of his head. "I don't think so."

**Order your copy of *Scripted To Slay* here -
books2read.com/scriptedtoslay**

HARVEY AND MARCUS'S BOOK RECOMMENDATIONS

Here, you will find all the books and authors recommended in *Tome To Tomb* to add to your never-ending to-read-list!

- *When The Bees Fly Home* by Andrea Cheng
- *The Quilts of Gee's Bend* by William Arnett
- *The Littlest Angel* by Charles Tazewell
- *When Breath Becomes Air* by Paul Kalanthi
- *On Death and Dying* by Elizabeth Kubler Ross
- *The Year of Magical Thinking* by Joan Didion
- *The Fault in our Stars* by John Green
- *The Diving Bell and the Butterfly* by Jean-Dominique Bauby
- The Nancy Drew Series - Carolyn Keene
- *Snow Day* by Billy Coffey
- *The Cat's Eye* by Margaret Atwood
- *Turtles All The Way Down* by John Green
- *Herzog* by Saul Bellow
- *A Visitation of Spirits* by Randall Kenan
- *Angle Of Repose* by Wallace Stegner

- *Santaland Diaries* by David Sedaris
- *Looking For Alaska* by John Green
- *All The Devils Are Here* by Louise Penny
- *Recipes for Love and Murder* by Sally Andrew
- *Between Boardslides* by Tony Hawk
- *Let's Take The Long Way Home* by Gail Caldwell
- *Stiff* by Mary Roach
- *The Beautiful Mystery* by Louise Penny

I recommend these books highly. Feel free to drop me a line at acfbookens@andilit.com and let me know if you read any or have books you think I should read. Thanks!

Happy Reading,

ACF

WANT TO READ ABOUT HARVEY'S FIRST SLEUTHING EXPEDITION?

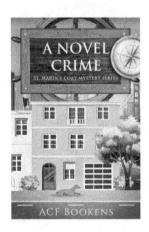

Join my Cozy Up email group for weekly book recs & a FREE copy of *A Novel Crime*, the prequel to the St. Marin's Cozy Mystery Series.

Sign-up here - https://bookens.andilit.com/CozyUp

ALSO BY ACF BOOKENS

Publishable By Death

Entitled To Kill

Bound to Execute

Plotted For Murder

Scripted To Slay - Coming January 2021

ABOUT THE AUTHOR

ACF Bookens lives in the Blue Ridge Mountains of Virginia, where the mountain tops remind her that life is a rugged beauty of a beast worthy of our attention. When she's not writing, she enjoys chasing her son around the house with the full awareness she will never catch him, cross-stitching while she binge-watches police procedurals, and reading everything she can get her hands on. Find her at bookens.andilit.com.

CPSIA information can be obtained
at www.ICGtesting.com
Printed in the USA
LVHW020049141222
735148LV00004B/591